To Jennie and Katie

Carissa Ann Lynch is the *USA Today* and *Wall Street Journal* bestselling author of *My Sister Is Missing*, *Without a Trace*, *Like Follow Kill*, *The One Night Stand*, *She Lied She Died*, *Whisper Island*, *The Secrets of Cedar Farm*, the *Flocksdale Files* trilogy, the *Horror High* series, *Searching for Sullivan*, *This Is Not About Love*, *Midnight Moss*, and *Shades and Shadows*. She resides in Floyds Knobs, Indiana, with her partner, children, and collection of books. With a background in psychology, she has always been a little obsessed with the darker areas of the mind.

carissaannlynch.wordpress.com

facebook.com/CarissaAnnLynchauthor
twitter.com/carissaannlynch
instagram.com/carissaannlynch_thrillers

Also by Carissa Ann Lynch

THE BACHELORETTE PARTY

CARISSA ANN LYNCH

One More Chapter
a division of HarperCollins*Publishers*
1 London Bridge Street
London SE1 9GF
www.harpercollins.co.uk
HarperCollins*Publishers*
1st Floor, Watermarque Building, Ringsend Road
Dublin 4, Ireland

This paperback edition 2022
1
First published in Great Britain in ebook format
by HarperCollins*Publishers* 2022
Copyright © Carissa Ann Lynch 2022
Carissa Ann Lynch asserts the moral right to be identified
as the author of this work
A catalogue record of this book is available from the British Library

ISBN: 978-0-00-855143-8

Printed and bound in the UK using 100% Renewable Electricity
by CPI Group (UK) Ltd

"There are a lot of places I like, but I like New Orleans better."

— Bob Dylan

Prologue

The detective walks through a tunnel of weepy oak trees, follows the picturesque path to the glowing French doors. She tries to imagine herself in the killer's shoes.

Did the killer sneak up on them? Or were they already inside when the party started?

She stares up at the strange, eclectic house. It inspires awe and horror in tandem.

The pediments and classic columns give the place an undeniable Greek feel. But like so many other domiciles in New Orleans, it's a haunting patchwork of influence— the Spanish and Caribbean flashes of color and design; the Creole parapets and cast-iron balconies; the Victorian motifs twisted like lace. And the siding looks Italian...

A true work of architectural genius… Too bad its reputation will be tainted after today, the detective thinks.

Someone has either decorated the front of the house for the bachelorette party, or it's left over from Mardi Gras; there are gaudy swoops of pearls and flowers, and massive bride and groom statues, which look to be made of papier-mâché, keep watch at the carriageway.

The detective stares at their faces; stoic, they reveal nothing about what transpired here. *What secrets are you hiding?* she wonders.

Through the carriageway, she stops at the French doors. Her assistant helps her into boot covers and gloves. He tucks her long dark hair into a rubbery hairnet.

The assistant is young and male, barely twenty. His eyes are frightened. His skin has turned a muted gray. But the detective pretends not to notice.

"Take me to her, please," she says.

Down a marbled hallway lined with a dark mix of Parisian and contemporary paintings, the assistant stops at the entry of a grand dining room and points toward the dining hall. It's large enough to fit a ballroom inside it.

On a long wooden table are the remnants of half-eaten food. The pungent aroma of rotting oysters fills the air. There are open wine bottles scattered from the head of the table on down.

The banquet assumes a substantial portion of the room, but the centerpiece of the space… is the woman.

The detective moves in, tiptoeing like a ghoulish ballet dancer around the ghastly main attraction.

The noose is tight around the victim's neck. She dangles from the rafters, still as a statue carved by Marcus Aurelius himself, as though she's part of the mishmash design that comes with the house, with this entire city…

The victim's eyes are open, staring.

The detective turns, follows her gaze toward the putrid food spread, trying to see through her victim's eyes. *What was the last thing you saw before you died? Or should I say:* who *did you see?*

There are others in the room—technicians, scouring for clues, but the detective might as well be alone with the dead woman. *What happened to you?* The detective's eyes comb the woman's body for answers. Hanging there, still and blank-faced she looks weightless…

Why did someone do this to you? And most importantly— who hated you enough to kill?

The detective walks a full circle around the victim, eyes never leaving the body. She nearly steps in a small puddle of blood before the assistant stops her.

Kneeling, she examines the coin-shaped blot on the marble floor, glancing back up at the victim.

The victim wears a long white dress, nearly see-through. No shoes. Her toenails are painted hot-pink.

The detective cannot say for certain until the medical examiner arrives, but she doesn't think the victim died by hanging.

"What are you thinking?" the assistant asks, mustering some fortitude despite his sickly pallor.

"Well, I can't say for sure. But I don't see much injury around the ligature. No scratch marks ... and she doesn't appear to have clawed at the noose. If someone strung you up like that, you'd fight like hell, wouldn't you?"

The assistant's face turns ashier.

"Maybe the victim put herself up there," he squeaks.

The detective shakes her head, slowly considering.

"Not a chance," she says, finally.

"Well, how do you know?"

The detective lifts an arm, points a latex finger at the back of the victim's head. "Can't see it too clearly from here, but she suffered from a head injury there on the back of her skull. The blood on the floor probably came from her, but this isn't where she was hit. A wound like that ... it would have caused a whole lot of mess, and I don't think the victim hit herself in the back of the head before hanging, do you? And how did she get herself up there? There's no stool or chair nearby..." The detective is talking at him, but she's mostly talking it through with herself.

She motions for one of the technicians and points at the blood on the floor.

Later, as the body is cut down and removed, the detective roams the halls of the mansion, room by room, taking it all in. She has had no luck finding a weapon.

A blow like that would have come from something hard... and from someone with a fast swing, she thinks inquisitively.

The detective imagines the perpetrator, lifting something heavy over the victim's head. She sees the weight of the blow, the whale-like moan someone might make after sustaining a sudden brain injury of that nature.

The detective's lieutenant has passed along some details already, but she wants to walk it through herself a few more times, the literal space and the scenario in her mind. She needs to get a feel of this place... She needs to know what happened, and how a joyous night could turn out so devastating. So tragic... so grisly.

Six women were present at the party and now one of them is dead.

The remaining five are in custody, secured and separated at the scene, and now awaiting questions down at the station. *Hopefully being managed with care until we have more information*, the detective thinks to herself.

The detective stops in the doorway of a massive library. Floor-to-ceiling shelves are crammed with heavy volumes and tomes. She prides herself on her eye for order. Whoever the caretaker of this place might be, they certainly have an eye for order too, she realizes.

The books are organized by height and width, the thickest and tallest volumes on the left, cascading from left to right, growing thinner and shorter, all the way to the smallest and narrowest volumes. It flows seamlessly… *perfectly*.

The detective's eyes roam the spines, left to right then down a row, right to left… It takes her less than a minute to find it—the chaos mingling with the order.

The offender is a thick red tome inched between two narrow tomes of the same height.

As she removes it, slowly and with care, she realizes the book isn't red at all. Rather, it is meant to be brown, but something has stained the corner of the heavy paperboard binding and leaked down the sides of it.

The detective turns it over and back, stares at the thick clump of hair and scalp attached to the sharpest edge. Her body jolts with surprise and revulsion.

"I need help in here," she whisper-shouts, hands shaky from the weight of the book, and the horror of what has happened here.

The detective's voice booms around the cavernous space, echoing back in her face. *This place feels less like a historical monument and more like an ill-fated tomb*, she thinks, hairs rising on the back of her neck for the first time all night.

Earlier, the detective saw pictures of the women: a fun-filled weekend, a celebration of what should have been one of the best moments in life, an event catalogued in real time with the help of social media and social influence...

But all the filters in the world can't hide this sort of darkness.

They could cover up their flaws and grievances with Gingham or Valencia filters, but no amount of lighting or special effects could change what one of them has done...

A monster in a pretty dress is still a monster.

Part One

~

"A little party never killed nobody."

— Fergie

Chapter One

The bride-to-be

The backyard of our new home spread out before me, stretching over a gentle slope then unfolding into a pasture. Beyond that, the land melted into a quiet hush of sugar maple trees and smudgy, rolling hills in every direction.

Two mares stood in the pasture, silent and watchful, unbothered by the eerie hush of falling snow. I stood at the edge of our veranda, weightless snowflakes brushing my cheeks and hands. I wondered if the horses were sleeping... *Do horses stand when they sleep or lie down?*

The smell of manure was strong, despite the cold, but the odor didn't bother me. The realtor had warned us when we walked the place, but the pasture smelled just fine to me—like farmland and fresh air. Like a fresh start for my tiny two-person family...

Asher and I had lived here for nearly a month now, but still, I hadn't adjusted. Half our belongings were stowed away in boxes, pushed aside in the deep dark corners of our three-bedroom farmhouse.

It's perfect, Asher told the real estate agent, before turning to me. *Isn't it perfect, Rosalee?*

What else could I say but 'yes', in that moment? I loved the farmhouse; this was true. And the way Asher's eyes lit up when he was excited about something, whether it was a big case he was working on at the law firm, or a story he'd read online; his eyes, warm and brown like pecans, would grow smiley and wide, like a kid bubbled over with Christmas morning delight.

Later, as the real estate agent typed up the deal, Asher repeated those words: *It's perfect*. Adding this: *For now.*

Us and a couple of kids. The perfect place to raise a family. Until we want to have even more kids, and we eventually outgrow the place, he had said.

I shivered at the memory. Yes, the house was perfect, and I loved my fiancé, but the thought of having so many kids we would soon outgrow it? That wasn't in the plans for me.

I loved the solitude of Moon County. The earthiness of dirt and manure. You could drive from one side of town to the other in thirty minutes, counting the crows and telephone wires, pointing out the silos and family farms that had obviously been around for generations. One generation gave way to the next, a bunch of knock-offs walking around, replacing the youth that came before them. We were all different here, yet all the same.

I loved it here, but also—I didn't feel settled. Not yet.

"You're freezing." Asher wrapped his thick arms around me from behind, squeezing me close to his chest. He smelled like aftershave and his favorite coffee, an over-priced bourbon barrel aged brew. He was wearing his thick, black, terrycloth robe. But still, I could feel his erection as he held me close. I shivered and pressed up against him.

"It seems wrong to go," I whispered, icy words forming foggy little puffs around my head. "We're just getting settled… and this is our first snow since moving…" Asher squeezed tighter, too tight, and I tried to relax, giving into the curve of his body, a shudder of pleasure running through me.

I didn't want to leave Asher—we hadn't spent a night apart from one another in ages.

Years ago, I developed a crush on him in middle school, but then I had to move away. It wasn't until I came back to Moon County that we had our first 'real' connection. But for me, my feelings for Asher had been going on for as long as I had hormones to act on. Even now, at twenty-eight, it felt surreal to think we were together. We were getting married soon—who would have thought?

Perhaps that could account for the unsettled lump in my chest, and that vile voice of self-doubt in my brain: We weren't married yet. He could still back out.

Asher laughed, a thick rumble in his chest that vibrated through me and turned my body warm all over. He had the best laugh. He might not have been perfect, but that laugh had always been one of his best features.

"Who are you kidding, Rosalee? You hate the snow."

True. Although he didn't exactly know why. Talk of my parents' fatal accident was something I avoided whenever possible, even with my future husband.

For me, the beauty of snow would always be intertwined with those ugly, dark days of death. That haunting silence snow brought, as though the entire world was vacuum-sealed and there was no one around to save you...

"And" Asher continued, "there's not that much left to unpack." *Lie.* The thought of all those boxes and all the sorting that needed doing, it overwhelmed all of my senses, the pressure thick in my chest to just *get it done, get it done...*

"What will you do without me though? You'll be lonely," I teased, my mood changing. I turned around, wrapping my arms around his waist, then lifting on my toes to kiss him. Even first thing in the morning, the milky sweetness of his skin and lips were enticing.

He rocked back on his heels playfully, then squeezed my face in his hands.

"Ah. Don't you worry about me. I have work to do on the Werner file and in my free time, I'll probably get drunk on cheap beer and start hanging some of your art on the walls," he grinned.

I groaned but smiled, unable to contain my pleasure. I wanted a place to hang my art pieces too, but if Asher had it his way, they'd be displayed front and center—in the living room or foyer, for all of our guests to see. I liked that he was proud of my work, but it also embarrassed me.

"Don't you dare. Wait until I come back at least," I said, taking one last longing glance toward the pasture. The horses were gone now, as though they'd never been there to begin with. My eyes drifted over to the gazebo next to the farmhouse; bright blue with tiny white pockets of flowers on its beams, it was one of my favorite features of the property.

I had suggested, casually, that perhaps we should hold the wedding here, in the gazebo. A simple ceremony on our lovely new patch of land...

Of course, Asher's mother nearly choked on her biscuit when I said that. "She's teasing Mom. Relax,"

Asher had said, rubbing smooth circles over his mother Elizabeth's back until her throat cleared.

"Well, I sure hope so. I've paid a fortune for Merribelle Gardens and already paid countless deposits on the flowers and caterers," she had huffed, refusing to meet my eye as she dabbed her lips with a fancy white linen napkin. That day, we had met for lunch at her favorite restaurant—a snobby, upscale place that charged a hundred dollars for a dab of meat with a smear of potatoes and a lettuce leaf on it.

I'd been horrified by it, even if she was the one paying the tab.

Ah yes—the grand Merribelle Gardens, the destination for our wedding this October.

Merribelle Gardens, and all the money my future mother-in-law had so generously put forth for our wedding. The whole grand plan had been her idea—a *tradition*, since she and Asher's late father had been married there in 1972.

I'd seen the glamorous pictures of their wedding day countless times. Elizabeth in her big ballgown with its floaty A-line and mother-of-pearl buttons... She had looked like a movie star. And Asher's father—tall and demure in his fancy black waistcoat with its classic pocket square.

There was no way Asher and I could live up to his mother's ideal wedding tradition.

It wasn't that I was opposed to getting married there. I just couldn't shake off the feeling that it was being held over my head, a constant reminder that I should feel grateful, *indebted* to the Beake family for simply letting me be a part of it.

My own parents weren't around to help pay for the wedding, and even if they had been, they were never as well off as Asher's family.

Whenever Elizabeth discussed the upcoming wedding, I often felt guilty, as though no matter how much I thanked her for planning and paying for it, and no matter how much enthusiasm I tried to muster, none of it was good enough. I suspected that she didn't like me. Dare I say, maybe even hated me.

And all my suggestions and ideas for the wedding were pushed aside... *How dare the peasant bride have an opinion, right?!*

I wasn't joking that day at the restaurant when I suggested the gazebo. I did love our new farmhouse, and the thought of having a small ceremony in my own mother's plain white dress with feet bare was appealing.

But I didn't want to disappoint Asher, and I certainly didn't want to disappoint his overly critical mother.

"Hey. Don't worry. Go! Have fun. You deserve this weekend. It's yours to celebrate," Asher said, shaking me out of my worried thoughts.

"Okay. If you insist," I sighed. Although, he and I

both knew, there was no way of getting out of New Orleans either. My best friend Mara had planned the bachelorette party; like Elizabeth, Mara wasn't opposed to using guilt and pressure to get her way.

Truthfully, I was excited to hang out with Mara. And the others… mostly. I'd never been to New Orleans and the thought of celebrating for a few days with friends in an authentic Greek Revival in the Garden District was too exotic to resist. It would be nice to get away for a few days, from the mess and stress of packing, from the wedding jitters and constant questions and answers from the wedding planners…

I needed a break from it all. The engagement, the home-buying process, the move—it was all too much for my historically fragile mental health.

Asher led me in through the back door, nudging me toward our bedroom to pack for the trip. "I'll make coffee and eggs. Maybe some pork sausage…" Even though the man worked ungodly hours at the law firm, he was a phenom in the kitchen when he offered to cook.

"Sounds wonderful." I kissed his cheek and drifted off to our room. My suitcase was under the bed, old and mostly unused. It had been years since I'd travelled anywhere.

Humming softly, I filled the soft fabric lining of the case with pockets of panties and bras, and my best T-shirts and jeans that had been unpacked. Despite the chilly weather here, the forecast in Louisiana looked perfect—a balmy seventy-nine degrees. I tossed in pajamas and a couple of old bathing suits in case there was a pool. I was tempted to try them on to see if they still fit, but I knew I'd get depressed about my weight gain. Over the last couple years, I'd put on nearly twenty pounds. Being in love and going out to eat all the time with your fiancé will do that, I guess. But it didn't make me feel very good when I tried to squeeze into undergarments or swimwear.

I'll just deal with trying on bathing suits when I get there, I decided, hastily.

After my clothes were all packed, I went in search of my tickets. They were in a folder, tucked away with all the airline details printed out by Mara and my cousin, Tinsley.

Where's that folder now, then? I wondered.

As I wandered down the hall to Asher's office, I could hear the sizzle of sausages and smell the warm scent of toast and coffee. My stomach grumbled.

Asher's office was still a work in progress, like the rest of the house. Housed in one of the spare bedrooms, he had a single desk and chair. The desktop was littered with files and folders. I spotted the neon yellow folder with my flight itinerary in it, balanced on a crooked stack of papers on the corner of the desk. He had obviously moved the folder into his office, thinking it was one of his.

I scooped up the folder and opened it, double checking my flight time and that everything I needed was there. Glancing at the other stack of papers on his desk, I was reminded of all the paperwork and drama that had been involved in buying our new, and first, home together.

Copies of our bank statements, tax forms, and every single asset we had ever owned. The only thing the mortgage lender didn't ask for was a picture of the inside of my underwear drawer...

I needed to go through these papers when I got back, file away the important ones and shred the duplicates.

I picked up the stack in my hands and straightened it, then set it back down neatly on the desk. I was about to turn away with my folder in hand, when my eyes drifted to a line item I hadn't noticed before on the top sheet of one of our bank statements.

Truthfully, I'd barely paid any of it any mind, just printing and printing and printing whatever the mortgage lender asked for.

Now, I picked the statement up, studying one of the bank charges listed at the very top. A recurring membership charge. For a place I knew all too well. A place Asher had no business going to...

In the kitchen, I held the folder to my chest like a

shield, watching the man I loved making breakfast. He glanced up at me and smiled, wagging the spatula playfully.

When I closed my eyes, I could see us there—on our first date. I'd always been intimidated by him as a young kid: his family's money, his confidence, his popularity, and his intimidating social circle. But then I ran into him at a local art fair, and the second he saw me, he waved and came strolling over, much to my surprise. *Rosalee, right? Long time, no see!* I was shocked that he remembered my name. We stood there in the park for an hour, leaning between rows of local artisans' tents, just talking. He spoke passionately about his law practice, but he wasn't one of those guys—like I had expected—who centered the conversation around himself. He asked questions about my life away from Moon County, about my art degree, my interests. A week later, he tracked me down on Facebook and asked me out on a proper date. I'd expected something classic, a fancy dinner or a trip to the local movie theater to see the new James Bond. But he surprised me with tickets to an art gallery in a neighboring city. He had seemed so thoughtful, so unexpectedly humble and kind, and over the years, his loyalty to me never seemed to waver.

Asher was my dream guy, not just his looks but his personality too. He was confident but caring, and he seemed to adore me. Which was why finding that bank charge made no sense.

I watched my future husband dance around the kitchen preparing my breakfast, wondering if I'd been wrong about him all along.

I thought I could trust him with my life, but perhaps that wasn't the case...

Chapter Two

ELIZABETH

The mother-in-law

"Are you sure about this? It's not too late to switch flights."

"Mom, stop it." My daughter, Bri, jabbed an elbow in my rib cage, but she was smiling when she did it. I knew she wanted to be here about as much as I did.

"Seriously. I have miles on my Amex. We could go anywhere you want. The Galapagos. Or, hey, what about Paris?" I teased.

I adjusted the backs of my diamond earrings, patted my neatly coifed bun. I was getting old, sure, my hair thinning and white, and my skin wrinkled as a prune, but I always strived to look my best, wearing expensive clothes in muted colors, and visiting my stylist once a month. I refused to be one of those lazy, old women walking around in a housedress and rollers.

"There she is." Bri spoke from the corner of her mouth, dipping her head toward my future daughter-in-law, Rosalee.

Rosalee stumbled through the terminal, catching herself just in time. She had a dented old suitcase swaying at her side.

"Good lord. Is that all she brought with her, that tiny suitcase?"

Bri's lips tightened; her thick brows furrowed together. "Looks like it, Mom."

I felt for her. Bri's baby brother was getting married when, in reality, it should have been her.

My daughter was beautiful, but different. Bri had her father's stature and face, his squarish jaw and thick, broad shoulders. And when she was angry, she looked like a linebacker perched for attack on the field. As much as I had wanted it for her—marriage, babies, a traditional life—it wasn't her thing. She was focused on her career building computers and creating her own custom models. I didn't understand a bit of it, but I always told myself I was proud of her. Even if I had to remind myself of it from time to time…

I am proud of my daughter, even if she doesn't choose to live her life the way I expected her to.

I zeroed in on my clumsy daughter-in-law-to-be as

she stopped in front of us. She dropped her suitcase at her feet and tugged on her stubby black ponytail, a line of sweat beading at her brow. *How can someone so young look so sweaty and out-of-breath all the time?* I wondered, and not for the first time.

"I went to the wrong terminal. And then I got hassled at security over the buckles on my shoes," Rosalee breathed.

Glancing down at her feet, I was horrified to see a pair of cheap Payless shoes that looked like a carryover from the nineties.

"They're comfortable," Rosalee said, following my gaze. "My mom always said to dress comfortably while traveling." She shrugged, then chewed her bottom lip— one awful habit out of many.

But I did feel a small lurch in my chest at the mention of her mother. It could not have been easy, losing her mother and father at such an early age. But surely, her mother could have taught her a thing or two about fashion, about walking with her head up and finding a sense of direction ... and about not wearing such ridiculous shoes.

Standing next to Bri and me, with our designer bags and expensive, yet *still comfortable*, shoes, Rosalee looked plumb ridiculous. I'd never been a flashy dresser— dressing like a Vegas showgirl isn't necessary for displaying wealth. But I liked classic designs and pantsuits.

I'd bet Rosalee didn't even own a nice pantsuit or dress shoes. How did she plan to attend dinners with Asher, when he met with clients and colleagues, if she didn't have a decent set of shoes?!

"Oh, I almost forgot! Here's your shirt." Bri beamed, as she thrust a folded pink T-shirt into Rosalee's hands. The words 'The Future Mrs. Beake' were embroidered in hideous sparkly gold letters on the front of it.

I couldn't help smiling as I watched Rosalee unfold the shirt and hold it up to her face. There was a flicker of something—a tiny clench in her jaw. But then she smiled brightly at Bri. "I love it! Thank you so much for making the shirts, Bri."

That flicker of annoyance, quickly masked with gratitude, came as no surprise to me. Rosalee's best friend and maid of honor, Mara, and her cousin, Tinsley, were in charge of throwing the bachelorette party. Yet my daughter Bri had insisted on overseeing the shirts from Day One. Bri had a close friend from high school who designed her own T-shirts—a cheesy endeavor, if you ask me—and she had promised to get them well-made, and at a reasonable price. But the others should have known, price isn't really something we worry about.

Mara had suggested something cute and classy—'Here comes the bride', 'Crown me'—and even a few funny inscriptions— 'Bride-zilla', 'Soon to be under new management'. But I was the one who pushed for 'The Future Mrs. Beake', and Bri had gone along with it too. She always listened to her mother.

It wasn't my fault Rosalee wanted to keep her own last name. Disgraceful, that's what it was. She should have been grateful to call herself a Beake now, especially considering the social standing the name would give her...

I'd expected an angrier reaction from her when she saw the shirt, but I should have known better—Rosalee was polite, if anything. Always biting her lip, being a try-hard when it came to impressing us and Asher. But I could see through her phony routine.

I watched in horror as Rosalee removed her thin jacket and started tugging the new T-shirt over the ratty one she was already wearing.

"Oh, you don't have to do that now..." Bri said, looking around at passers-by, embarrassed.

"No, I want to! Thanks again for this. I just adore it. Your friend who makes these is very talented," Rosalee beamed, struggling to pull the T-shirt over her breasts and flabby stomach. She wasn't a heavy girl, but she certainly wasn't in shape. Last year I bought her a pair of maternity pants for Christmas, hoping she would take the hint. Instead, she had thanked me and promised to wear them soon. Knowing her and her fashion sense, she probably did wear them...

"Where are the others?" I sniffed, looking at my favorite watch with its diamond band. It was a present from Edmund on our twenty-fifth anniversary. I blinked back memories of that day, his cheesy grin, slipping the velvet box across the table before I'd even taken a bite of my dinner. He'd always been so impatient when it came to gift-giving. He loved the thrill of seeing me open things, watching my eyes sparkle with the presents he bestowed upon me. Despite all his showiness and spoils, he was never a man who cared about buying things for himself. His favorite thing to wear was holey pajama pants and he didn't even own any jewelry. *Edmund probably would have loved Rosalee,* I thought, a flicker of annoyance running down my spine as I continued to watch her struggle with the too-tight shirt.

"Georgia's almost here. Not sure about the other two…" Bri said, face bent down over her phone, trying not to look at Rosalee's scuffle with the shirt.

"You talked to Georgia?" Rosalee asked breathily. Now she was attempting to stretch out the tight cotton away from her bulging waistline. I'd wondered a couple of times if she could be pregnant. In my mind, I'd fantasized about the way she and Asher would break the news to me—a fancy cake with a hidden message inside or a gift that when opened would reveal the grainy ultrasound portrait of my first grandchild…

Rosalee wasn't the daughter-in-law I'd hoped for but

having a grandchild on the way... That would have changed everything. The clock was ticking; I wasn't getting any younger and I hoped to still have some energy for a grandchild someday...

"Yeah. Georgia texted me about an hour ago. She should be here by now," Bri said casually, eyes still glued to her phone.

My eyes wandered over Rosalee's face, the pained expression at the mention of Georgia's name. I'd made no secret of the fact that I thought it would be Georgia standing here—more toned and better dressed than Rosalee—serving as the bride-to-be for Asher. Asher and Georgia had been thick as thieves since grade school. Georgia's mother and I were lifelong friends; as children, Asher and Georgia were always running together, keeping themselves entertained with pirate and war games, while Mary and I sipped gin and tonics and gossiped about the men in our lives.

In middle school and high school, Georgia and Asher had developed into miniature adults. Georgia blossomed and grew prettier, and Asher shot up like a flower, towering over her and all his classmates. He was destined to play sports and, all through school, he made friends wherever he went. Any girl would have been lucky to have Asher Beake, but he never left Georgia's side. They rode to school together every morning and afternoon. They spent time together on the weekends.

For a long time, I just assumed they were dating, it was only natural. I didn't even know Rosalee existed back then and I don't think Asher did either. It wasn't until she moved back to town later that I really got to know the girl...

After high school, Asher left for law school and Georgia left to study for a degree in nursing; they drifted apart, and Asher met other women, sometimes bringing them home for breaks or holidays. None of them measured up to Georgia. Not even close.

When Rosalee moved back to town and she and Asher started dating, it became obvious that it was more than a short-lived fling. For some reason that I couldn't quite grasp, my son was enamored by Rosalee. He laughed and smiled every time she was around, and seemed unbothered by her plain, messy appearance.

Finally, I had asked him—what was the deal with Georgia? By then, she was done with nursing school; like Asher, she had come back home to her family and roots. Why were they not pursuing something romantic? Why did he choose the frumpy Rosalee over the girl he'd known all his life, Georgia?

Ah mom. You know me and Georgia have always just been friends. I don't think of her in that way, and she doesn't either, Asher had said.

But he was wrong—I could see it in Georgia's eyes when he told her the news about Rosalee. Georgia was jealous about his upcoming marriage, she had to be. I only wished she would try to stop him, stop this whole ridiculous charade before it was too late...

"There she is! Hello, darling!" I squealed, mustering all the excitement I could. It wasn't hard when it came to Georgia, my greeting totally at odds with how I had greeted Rosalee earlier.

Georgia approached us gracefully, her Coach carry-on in the crook of her arm and an extra-large, matching suitcase rolling beside her. She set her luggage down and opened her arms, embracing me in a too-long hug. She smelled like honeydew and toothpaste; as usual, she looked like a girl who, although humbly and smartly dressed, could have been a runway model. Thick blond hair, beachy waves. Long, striking eyelashes that were clearly extensions, but could probably pass for real ones. When she smiled, she showed all her teeth. And, as I glanced down at her feet, I noted her espadrilles—she had better taste in shoes, that's for sure.

Georgia extracted herself from our embrace and turned to Rosalee. "Hi there! Congratulations! I'm so excited for this trip. Thank you for letting me come, and for asking me to be a bridesmaid," Georgia beamed. She put her arms around Rosalee, who looked startled as she settled into the embrace. That was one thing that Georgia and Rosalee had in common—they were both too nice. I just wished she'd run Rosalee off and stake her claim on my son. Lord knows they looked more suited for one another, and they were both enthusiastic about their careers. Unlike Rosalee, with her strange and eerie paintings, the dusty spots of chalk on her clothes and face whenever I stopped by for a visit…

"Aw, it's my pleasure. Thank you for agreeing to be a bridesmaid. You're Asher's best friend, so it only makes sense…" Rosalee said. She closed her mouth then opened it, then closed it again, as though she had something else to say but couldn't.

As Bri handed over Georgia's shirt—nicer and well-fitted, for certain—I watched Rosalee study my son's best friend. It was no surprise Georgia intimidated her.

Good. She should be intimidated. She should be afraid of us all, I thought, slyly.

Chapter Three

MARA

The best friend

My eyes wandered from one woman to the next as I approached with my shiny black carry-on bag. I had many flaws, but if there was one thing I was good at, it was reading a room. Rosalee's awful soon-to-be in-laws, the beak-nosed Mrs. Beake and her thunderous daughter Bri looked downright miserable, waiting in their neatly-pressed designer pants, silky button-downs, and over-priced flats. *Did they plan out their outfits together in advance? Ew,* I thought, leerily.

And *Georgia. The* fucking Georgia. Don't get me started on her...

Georgia is the bane of my best friend Rosalee's

existence. Rosalee didn't tell me that, but then again, she didn't need to. Best friends know these things.

When your fiancé's 'best friend' is a woman who looks like an Instagram model, there's nothing left to do but hate. And me, being me, can't help hating anyone who upsets my closest friend from college.

Call me old-fashioned, but women and men aren't friends. If they are, it's only because one of them wants more and the other doesn't.

Georgia made no sense to me...

For the life of me, I couldn't understand it—Rosalee had asked me to be her maid of honor (obviously), and I could understand having Tinsley as a bridesmaid too. Tinsley was Rosalee's only cousin and Tinsley's family had taken her in after the tragic loss of her parents. Me and Tinsley—we made sense. And Tinsley had at least proven herself to be useful, covering most of the party costs on her own. But why did Rosalee have to ask Bri and Georgia to be bridesmaids too?

I'd had no choice but to invite the other two bridesmaids to the bachelorette party... and then Rosalee had also insisted we ask Elizabeth, the matriarch of the Beakes, with her poufy white hair and long nose, perfect to look down on you with.

Frankly, my best friend was being way too nice. The party was supposed to be about her, *for her*—not a way to kiss up to her future in-laws and her husband's female 'bestie'. If I'd had it my way, we would have invited our closest acquaintances from our college days and had a wild shindig, stress-free.

But Rosalee wanted this, and as the party thrower, it was my job to meet her demands.

I was determined to make this bachelorette party not only a weekend to remember, but the best fucking weekend of Rosalee's life.

My best friend is getting married, and she deserves this. She deserves to feel celebrated.

I just wished she would have chosen some kinder participants...

Rosalee looked so awkward and unsure of herself standing in that group of women; I just wanted to squeeze her up and dropkick those bitches around her. Especially Georgia.

"Ladies!" I launched my bag toward their inner circle and slid my owlish sunglasses down my nose. "Who's ready for the best fucking weekend of their life?"

Elizabeth's mouth fell open and Bri narrowed her eyes at me. And I didn't even bother looking at Georgia. Lord knows I'd studied her enough on the Gram already.

"Elizabeth and Bri! So lovely to finally meet Asher's family in person!" I squealed with mock delight.

Elizabeth offered me a matronly hand; her wedding ring sparkled like a firecracker, gaudy yet wonderful. I hated her for it. Ignoring the hand, I reached for my best friend's future mother-in-law, and squeezed her perfectly narrowed waistline so hard she let out a small 'umph'. As much as it killed me to admit it, Elizabeth Beake was hot for an old lady. She dressed to impress in sharp clothes and expensive jewels, putting out old money vibes without even trying to.

Bri, the sister, was big and brutish, too hard to get my arms around. But she was well-dressed and expensively dressed like her mother. I gave her a light hug with a hard slap on the back. Despite the plastered smile, her face was disdainful. These Beake women were exuding *hate vibes*. I could see why they intimidated Rosalee.

Lucky for me, I don't get shaken so easily.

Next, I turned to Georgia. "Ummm… I'm so sorry. It's early and I haven't had my coffee. Joanna, right?"

"Georgia," Elizabeth snapped before Georgia could even answer.

"Georgia, Georgia…!" I belted out the words to that timeless Ray Charles song, startling a few huffy travelers passing by. "I bet you hear that all the time, right?" I teased.

When Georgia smiled, it was like her whole face smiled with her. Her eyes were pale green, her face dewy and smooth as a skincare commercial, her lips soft and small like a perfect rose bud. Even though I hated to admit it, this one exuded *sweetness*.

"Oh, you wouldn't believe how often people start

singing my name! When I was younger, I found it annoying, but now it's kind of endearing. It is a good song, after all. They could always sing something worse, I guess," Georgia said.

"Right. Like, 'Jolene, Jolene, Jolene…'" I belted, clapping out the beat on my thigh with one hand.

If Georgia caught my drift, she didn't show it. Instead, she said, "Well, it's awfully nice to meet Rosalee's best friend. Finally! Asher's told me so much about you."

Asher, huh?

"Hopefully, only the good things," I said, turning toward my best friend. Why was Georgia talking to Asher about me? Sure, I'd spent some time with Rosalee's fiancé, but it wasn't like he knew me all that well either…

"Come here, you." I took my best friend in my arms, squeezing and tugging until I'd lifted her off her feet. "Wait. What the hell is this? Did they order a kid's size by accident?" I let her go and tugged on that disastrous bridal party shirt. Bri had insisted on being in charge of the shirts. But I knew this would happen. Luckily, I'd come prepared.

"Oh, it's not so bad. It's cute, just a little tight…" Rosalee tugged at the waist, trying to stretch the material out around her stomach.

"Oh, now you're just being nice! It's definitely too

small and looks cheaply made, too. I guess it could be worse. At least they didn't accidentally pick up a maternity size!" I let out a loud, raucous chuckle, then turned to lock eyes with Elizabeth. *Yes, of course my best friend told me about the maternity debacle at Christmas. And yes, I predicted that you and your daughter wouldn't do a respectable job with the shirts today, either…*

"Don't worry, sweetie, I picked up some gorgeous black and purple pre-made shirts at Barney's last weekend. I have one for you right here in my bag. Let's go to the bathroom and take that one off…"

Rosalee's cheeks turned apple-red.

"Come on," I insisted. Locking arms, I steered her in the direction of the airport bathrooms.

Over my shoulder, I flipped a look at Bri beaming her with my best "fuck you, bitch" smile.

They could try all they want to ruin my best friend's party and her impending marriage, but I won't let them. Nobody was hurting Rosalee this weekend, unless over my dead body…

"Thank you," Rosalee muttered, once we were safely tucked in the stall. She lifted the too-tight shirt over her head as I unfolded the new one and handed it to her. She seemed tense and distracted, her shoulders and jaw tight. Her eyes were far away and sleepy. Was it just the drama and anxiety of dealing with her in-laws or was it something more? There was a stiffness to her that I hadn't seen in a long time, like she was going through the motions but not really present.

"Are you okay? I'm sorry about the shirt. I should have insisted on doing that myself too…"

"I'm fine." Rosalee slid the new purple shirt over her head and adjusted her stubby black ponytail.

I shoved the other shirt in the tampon can, and watched my best friend's reflection in the bathroom mirror. She lifted her lips, trying to force a smile. Watching her made me feel a sudden rush of sadness.

'Lucky in love', the shirt read, the 'o' fashioned into a glittery engagement ring. But was she truly lucky, I couldn't help wondering? *Yes, she's marrying the guy she's coveted since grade school, but is it worth it if she has to deal with those terrible in-laws?*

"You sure you're okay? Was everything fine with Asher when you left?" I reached up and adjusted her ponytail for her in the mirror. One thing I loved about Rosalee—she was never fake, and she liked to dress for comfort. Sure, she could dress up more from time to time and she'd put on a few extra pounds since getting engaged, but she would always be a hottie in my book. Screw those mean bitches for trying to ruin her day from the get-go!

"Yeah. Everything's fine. But where is Tinsley? I figured y'all would show up together since you planned the party together..." Rosalee said, shifting out of my grasp.

I took a deep breath through my mouth and blew it out like a bull through my nose. I'd been dreading this moment. "Yeah, about that... Tinsley isn't coming. I'm sorry."

Chapter Four

The cousin

It wasn't that I was afraid of flying. I just didn't like the crowds or the claustrophobia, stuck with all those tightly compacted bodies 40,000 feet in the air.

If anyone could understand my fears, it was my cousin, Rosalee. We had practically grown up together as sisters, her coming to live with me and my mother at the age of fourteen after her parents died.

The drive to New Orleans was grueling, but I relished the time alone in my Prius, listening to audiobooks and blasting my favorite old songs from the nineties. Not only did I make it on time, but by the time I backed into my long-term parking slot, I was hours early.

A shiny black Uber was there waiting to pick me up.

I'd booked it prior to leaving on the voyage, and I couldn't have timed my arrival more perfectly.

"What's going on? You must be Tinsley," the driver said with a big flashy smile, rolling his window all the way down. It wasn't my first time visiting The Big Easy, but I'd forgotten the beauty of its accents—this man's vowels were round and smooth like cobbles in a stream.

"That's me. Let me grab my bag." I double and triple checked my door locks, then switched my luggage over to his car.

"Let me get that for you. On in." He opened the back door for me, and I slid in, grateful for the air conditioning and the soft, cool seats. It might have taken me half a night and a day's drive to get here, but at least I'd avoided the plane and all those people. I just hoped Rosalee wasn't too disappointed.

The drive had been strange, chilly temperatures fading away when I reached Birmingham, and the moisture thickening as I drew further south. The air in New Orleans felt sticky and airless, settling over my skin like a layer of soup.

"What brings you to New Orleans?" he asked, although when he said it, it sounded like 'Nyoo Ahhlyins'. I smiled politely at his bright white teeth in the rearview.

"Bachelorette party for my cousin. Though she's more like a sister really…"

"Ah! You missed Mardi Gras. Too bad," he said, pulling away from my Prius. As he swooped into traffic onto a busy, colorful street, I watched my car disappear in the rearview mirror.

"Yeah, too bad. My cousin, Rosalee, she wanted to avoid the carnival crowds," I said. Mardi Gras was over, but you couldn't tell it—beads still clung to porch rails and remnants of bright awnings, balloons, and streamers were displayed on the houses and shops. The sidewalks were busy with people, some dressed as brightly as the colorful buildings beside them.

Awestruck, I watched the multi-colored buildings swish by—there was no separation between them, as though the entire city were connected, one long heaping heart, each artery pumping blood to the next chamber.

Perhaps it was age that helped me see it clearer now; I was barely twenty-one when I came here last, and the whole place looked different now. The Gothic-inspired moldings and lacy wrought iron, the shotguns next to the Creole cottages—this amazing patchwork of French, Spanish, and Caribbean influences meshed into this unbelievable tapestry. *There's no other place quite like it, that's for sure.*

"Leblanc and Landry, right?" the driver asked, breaking the spell that had overcome me.

"That's the one." The Leblanc-Landry mansion was in the Garden District, close enough to Bourbon Street and the festivities of downtown, but also with an air of seclusion on its acre of land surrounded by tremendous old oak trees.

Mara and I had pored over the pictures dozens of times, planning and planning. Well, it was mostly her—I just nodded and went along with whatever she said. I'd quickly learned that there was no 'team' in teamwork with Rosalee's best friend Mara; she ran the show and you either assisted or got the hell out of her way.

Leblanc-Landry was secluded and romantic, with its hidden courtyard, freakish old trees, and cotton-candy architecture—it was perfect, all but the price. When I'd agreed to help plan Rosalee's bachelorette party, I hadn't agreed to foot the bill.

Mara had promised to pay me back before the trip—I'd put most of it on my credit card. But here I was, in New Orleans… and she still hadn't paid me. Mara, with all her trendy clothes and accessories, the pricey makeup and designer haircut, without a dollar to her name, apparently. There were so many excuses—she needed to 'move some money around first'; she was waiting for an owed payment from her employer; she lent too much to her sick relatives…

I'd heard it all from Mara over the last few months. At first, I'd been inclined to believe her. But then she never paid me back. And despite running up the bill in my name, she spared no expense for the party, either.

I had to face it. I'd probably be stuck with my three nearly maxed out credit cards while Mara got all the credit for the party from Rosalee and the other attendees...

Unlike Mara, I wasn't a trust fund kid with a degree to fall back on. I had to work for every penny I earned at my job and her thoughtlessness when it came to paying me back was enough to make me clench my teeth every time I conjured up her face or name...

I took a deep breath, counting backwards, forcing myself to push aside the thought of money for this one weekend to focus on my dear cousin Rosalee. We had practically grown up together, sharing so many moments and memories. It was hard to believe she was getting married.

Closing my eyes, I could see us there, fourteen and fabulous, wrapping our bodies in sheets and fashioning tiaras out of weeds from my mother's garden. We held fake wedding ceremonies and chanted whimsical vows, playacting adulthood.

Oh, if only adulthood were as fun and easy and magical as we made it seem back then...

The hodgepodge heartbeat of the city grew softer as the buildings and townhouses faded away. Around a sharp bend and over a small hill, I saw the mansion. It was set back from the road, a massive bleeding heart at the end of a crooked lane. Even from here, I could see the statues and decorations we had ordered for the party on display in the carriageway. The décor that *I* paid for, not Mara.

The driver flipped his signal and turned down the long driveway.

"So, what are y'all's plans for the weekend? Going to get wild?" the driver asked, his eyes watchful and animalistic in the rearview mirror.

"No… I don't know. I'm sure we'll visit some local nightspots and get a feel of the city," I said, tearing my eyes away from his and looking eagerly toward the mansion they were approaching.

"Well, why don't you and your friends call my number if you need a ride? Or if you're looking to party, me and some of my boys can come by. A big mansion like that, you got plenty of room for a big party," the driver said.

"If you don't mind," I said, placing my hand on the handle, "I think I'll get out and walk from here. If it's okay with you…"

"You sure? I don't mind carrying your bag inside, especially considering the generous tip…"

"No, that won't be necessary. I'd like to take the walk and carry my own bags," I insisted, eager to escape from him. "Thank you so much for bringing me though." I'd left a tip for him on the Uber app, but I handed him an extra twenty and forced a smile.

"Don't forget what I said. I can show you ladies a good time," he said, glancing at the mansion as though he might try to come inside right now.

"Okay. Sure." I took the business card he was offering and hopped out.

"Thanks again... Henry," I said, glancing at the card, then slammed my door shut with a thud.

After collecting my bag, I watched Henry pull away. *I definitely won't be calling him for a ride again*, I thought, with a small shudder.

I turned to look at the mansion, relieved that I was all alone again. It was a beautiful place, in an eclectic, other-worldly way, although I would have gone without the cheesy decorations strewn out front if it were up to me instead of domineering Mara.

I approached slowly, bag swinging beside me, taking in the massive trees, most of which were between 600 and 900 years old. I'd done my research on this place online. While Mara was busy worrying about the linens, culinary delicacies, and amenities, I was reading everything I could on the Leblanc-Landry estate.

There were stories and rumors about this place... voodoo and murder. But there were many places like that in New Orleans. The difference with this one was that it was supposedly haunted. A couple of amateur ghost-hunting crews from YouTube had turned out years ago, catching some interesting footage for their channel.

Most normal people would shy away from this place, I knew Mara certainly would if she knew. But I wasn't normal. I wasn't *most* people. The dark and macabre attracted me… and this place had been speaking to me ever since I first laid eyes on the grainy photos online.

Some of the ghost hunters called this place 'evil'. But when you grow up in the buckle of the Bible Belt, you're taught to fear fire and brimstone before you're even out of diapers, nothing scares you anymore.

This house felt like the perfect place to reconnect with Rosalee and make sure she wants to marry this man. And while I was here, why not enjoy the creepy location, too? Perhaps I could catch a ghost sighting or two of my own and submit it to my favorite YouTubers…

The pearls and beads strewn over the awning were pretty and tasteful, but I scowled at the overgrown bride and groom. Facing each other on either side of the entranceway steps, their faces were puckered, not as though they were preparing to kiss, but rather, they looked to be holding their breath, as though caught in the middle of a tense argument…

I knocked on the heavy French doors, wondering if I was too early. The caterers and support staff were scheduled to arrive before the bride-to-be and her group's arrival, but they probably hadn't expected me to turn up three hours early.

I knocked again, then placed my hand on the brass doorknob. The door creaked open, startling me.

"Hello?" I popped my head around the door but saw no one on the other side of it. Stepping inside, I closed the door behind me and set my suitcase on the floor against the foyer wall.

The foyer was dark. No natural light seeped in, the windows high and foggy, despite the late afternoon hour. Candles burned on either side of the entry, casting wavy glows from their sconces, making the eccentric oil paintings and designs on the aging wallpaper look strange and menacing.

"Hello?" I called out again, my voice ricocheting through a long dark hallway. I followed the candlelight, gasping as I entered a grand ballroom—no, not a ballroom, a dining room. The long-slabbed table and high-backed chairs reminded me of something medieval: a table fit for a king and his retinue.

Finally, I heard noises—the clank of metal on glass, the sizzle of someone's cooking. I followed the symphony of sounds, finding my way through two metal swinging doors that led to an industrial-sized kitchen. Half a dozen chefs were hard at work rolling dough for desserts, bowling crab legs, and slicing vegetables and cheese for salads.

"Hello! You must be Mara!"

I jumped at the sound of a voice beside me, turning

quickly towards an elderly, stout woman dressed all in black. She was wearing a shiny gold nametag. *Delfina.*

"No, I'm Tinsley. Mara is the other friend planning the party." I stuck out my hand and she took it.

"Tinsley … I don't think we've spoken. It's mostly been Mara, going back and forth in our email exchanges."

I frowned. "Yes, that's right. Of the two of us, she's definitely the one in charge of handling communication. But I'm the one footing the bill." I couldn't resist letting her know.

"Oh." Delfina shifted her matronly hips and gave me an uncomfortable smile. She looked like Betty Crocker, with her old-fashioned apron and starched-white uniform. She had to be nearly seventy or eighty years old.

"The others flew, but I drove. I'm sorry if I arrived too early. I just couldn't help myself. This place is simply marvelous," I breathed, watching the workers float effortlessly around the kitchen as though they were following a carefully choreographed dance.

"Oh, no problem at all!" Delfina grinned. "We are so grateful to have you. We get so many revelers and tourists during Mardi Gras. It's nice to have a proper party to tend to. I'm pleased to have you," she said curtly. She seemed friendly but proper, and I could tell that she was the one in charge by the way she watched the others moving through the kitchen with a hawklike stance.

"Well, thank you for letting us do it here and agreeing to host the dinner. How can I help?"

Delfina waved me off. "No need for anything. I have it all taken care of. The bedrooms are on the second floor. Each room has been pre-selected, and you should easily find yours. Dinner will be served at seven, not a moment sooner…"

"Thanks again, Delfina."

Once outside the kitchen, I went back and retrieved my suitcase. But instead of going up to the bedrooms, I wandered around the first-floor rooms. The dining and sitting rooms were better lit than the entrance, vintage chandeliers glittering like diamonds in every room I passed. Everything looked clean, but vintage—the heavy cream curtains, the weird portraits, odd ceramic sculptures, and knick-knacks spread in every open crevice and corner.

Through the back window, I could see the pavilion—a cobbled courtyard filled with wrought-iron café tables, bright yellow string lights strewn through the trees and along the brick archways… like its own little slice of Paris. It was still daylight, yet the lights were on, the secluded brick barriers giving it a dark, intimate feel.

Through an archway, I could see the part of the estate that had Mara's name written all over it. An inground pool surrounded by modern loungers, and a steamy hot tub under a palm tree and surrounded by thick, private shrubs. *I didn't even realize there were palm trees in New Orleans*, I thought, dreamily.

This place truly was an odd mixture of old and new, strange and familiar, sort of like the exterior designs of the house and surrounding city. A city where you go to feel connected, found. But at the same time, it seemed like the sort of place where you could blend in and, eventually, disappear if you wanted to. Outside Mardi Gras, there was no separation between tourists and locals —just a blending of peoples.

I shook away my thoughts, feeling strangely sleepy. Perhaps I'd lie down and rest a bit before the others arrived...

But on the way to the grand, second-floor staircase, I ran into more distractions.

Jaw-dropping chandeliers and a fancy bathroom bigger than my bedroom back home, fitted with pedestal sinks and more chandeliers. A lavish sunroom filled with Turkish rugs and well-worn, but well-loved, sofas and loveseats.

I stopped and took a short breath when I found the library.

"Jesus Christ." The walls were lined floor to ceiling with heavy books. In the center of the room, were several leather reading chairs and tiny tables that offered old-fashioned glass ashtrays. *If this were my library, I'd kill some one for smoking in it,* I thought, peevishly.

The books were also vintage—Dickens and Twain, Shakespeare and Faulkner. As much as I loved the old-worldly feel of this place, I felt like the books were trying too hard. There was nothing wrong with classics, but if this were my library, I'd have filled it with new, modern titles. Feminist and edgy. I'd have put every banned book I could find on the lowest and easiest to reach shelves.

I was tempted to borrow a book or two, but they were so perfectly arranged, it would certainly be noticeable if I did so. I'd ask Delfina later. Maybe the books could be checked out somehow, or at the very least I could park myself right here in this room when I needed a break from the others, and do some reading in one of those luxurious chairs…

My eyes grew heavier just thinking about it, the exhaustion from the long drive and the overly pushy driver bearing down on my shoulders and chest. My eyelids felt weighty as I made my way back out through the long dark hallway and up the double-sided staircase that led to the second-floor bedrooms.

The second floor was less grand than the first, but I preferred it—the walls painted a soft, eggshell-blue at the bottom, curly bits of flower and ivy wallpaper stretching to meet the ceiling above. Precisely six bedrooms—it couldn't be a more perfect set-up for Rosalee's bachelorette party. Almost as though we were destined to come here…

Through the long, airy hallway, I peeked in, room by room, looking for mine. As planned, each private room came equipped with its own lush bathrobe on the bed, each guest's name stitched in gold lettering on the right breast. *I wonder how much each of these cost me*, I thought, bitterly, rolling my eyes when I saw the one with Mara's name etched in gold. I didn't understand what Rosalee saw in Mara, I truly didn't. She was self-centered and annoying. But that wasn't true—I did understand it because I understood Rosalee. Unlike me, with my hermit-like tendencies and withdrawn personality, Rosalee could shine in a crowd. She knew how to fake it; in fact, I'd watched her do it for years after her parents died. And an outgoing person like Mara was exactly the type of friend Rosalee had always been drawn to…

Rosalee was fourteen when she came to live with me and my mother. To say I wanted her there would be an epic lie. I didn't want her to come at all.

Rosalee's father was my mother's brother, but I'd only met them once previously, before that fateful day when Rosalee lost both mother and father in the span of a few short hours.

Mom didn't ask me if it was okay; rather, she told me that Rosalee was coming. Not to stay for a while, but to live permanently. And she expected me to treat her with care. *I want you to do better than kindness, Tinsley. I want you to shower her with love. Make her feel at home. Just think of her as the sister you always wanted but never had*, my mother insisted.

But that's just it—I'd never wanted a sister either.

Dad died of a stroke when I was six; my memories of him were mostly non-existent. A stick-figure man who I filled in myself, each time making him fuller and more colorful, and over time, my imagination altered the course of my memories forever.

When you lose someone at that age, your memory of them—your idea of them, really—is just a hodgepodge of other people's stories. His old bomber jackets in the coat closet, the smell of tobacco and Old Spice embedded in the fabrics tucked in the boxes in the dark corner of the basement. Pictures... So many of them. Just a face and a body—no one I knew, not really.

For as far back as I could remember, it was just my mom and me. We lived alone in our three-bedroom townhouse; we ate easy meals together, like grilled cheese and tomato soup, or pink salmon from a can.

I enjoyed our dinners. Tucked away at our two-seater table or curled up thigh to thigh on the loveseat watching old episodes of *Cheers* or *The Brady Bunch*.

Occasionally, I complained of boredom. I made few friends and Mom made even fewer in her grown-up world, working at the local mortuary. *My co-workers are a bunch of stiffs*, she would say at school functions, a recycled joke for the other parents—a punchline no one seemed to understand or appreciate. But I did.

Honestly, I wasn't all that bored. I enjoyed her company at that age more than I cared to admit. Mostly, I enjoyed being tucked away in my room, with the company of my books., My idea of an epic weekend was reading Mom's old Harlequin romance novels or classic mysteries.

So, when Rosalee Mumford moved into our house, blood or not, I was annoyed by her presence. She was like Stella Starr from *Space Invaders*, this sexy marauder with her full breasts to my flat chest, her wild drawings and painting habits... her abhorrence for reading.

I hated her those first few days. We had a spare room she could have used, but Mom insisted on keeping that space to herself for sewing and praying, so after a lifetime of living as an only child with my own space, my room was suddenly rearranged. Bunk beds and an extra dresser, half the normal space for my clothes and, most importantly, my precious books.

But something happened that first summer with Rosalee... We might have been different, our personalities, but we connected in a way I'd never anticipated.

She had dreams, nightmares really. And after a few nights of tossing and turning, screams and shouts, she asked if she could get in bed with me. I guess most people would have thought it was strange—two fourteen-year-old girls crowded together on a twin-sized mattress. I certainly thought it was strange at first.

But for the first time since her arrival, Rosalee slept. She curled her calves around mine, like interlocking pieces, and I watched her breathing, short puffy breaths that made her curly-cue bangs float out when she exhaled.

My cousin was beautiful. And damaged. I couldn't imagine losing my mother. Sure, I'd lost Dad, but I'd been too young to feel it. To understand it fully at the time.

Late-night sleeping sessions became late-night confessions. Rosalee told me her secrets and I told her mine. I read her pages from my stories, and she painted a picture of me, making me look beautiful in a way I'd never seen or felt before.

We spent the daytime hours outdoors, walking to the public pool or park or riding bikes. I'd never really had a friend before. But more than that—she felt like a sister, just like Mom had said.

I expected it all to change when school started. And in a way, things did evolve.

Rosalee wasn't considered the prettiest girl, but she was new and had lost something, and that intrigued people. Plus, Rosalee was always nice. She fitted in with both boys and girls alike.

Despite all that, she never left my side. She never made me feel like a leper, and as a result, the kids at school were kinder, and included me, along with Rosalee.

Middle school advanced to high school. Rosalee joined drama and I joined nothing, spending my free time reading and writing. Mom pushed me to join more things like Rosalee, but Rosalee defended me. *I wish I were smart and had the patience for reading like Tinsley. If I did, I wouldn't be running around trying to find extra things to keep me busy,* she told her.

The closer I got to Rosalee and my school friends, the farther I got from Mom. I guess that's what happens when you become a teenager. Things change, and maybe they're supposed to.

I didn't know Mom had cancer; she knew but never told us, and to this day, I feel angry at her for not giving me a chance to deal with it, to say some sort of formal goodbye...

Rosalee and I were both nearly eighteen by then; a distant uncle we barely knew on my father's side came to stay with us for a brief time. Then Rosalee left for college, and I spent my days missing my mother. And I missed Rosalee, too.

I thought it would be me going off to study, to write books, or to get a degree in library science. But it was

Rosalee who left town, and I was the one who stayed. Left behind with Uncle Noah. I got a job at the local bookstore and tried my best to cope with depression and grief. I missed Mom so terribly, and although I'd never admit it to anyone, I missed Rosalee even more.

We stayed in contact—phone calls and texts. A few letters. But it wasn't the same.

I became a full-fledged adult and Uncle Noah moved out. All that was left was me and all those empty rooms, the ghosts of my mother and pseudo-sister to keep me company.

When Rosalee finally finished college and moved back to Moon County, she didn't come home to me. She got her own apartment and things just weren't the same between us. She had brand new friends, like Mara.

Perhaps part of me resented her for that—for pulling me away from my mom, holding me in her orbit for so long, and then flinging me out into space, all alone, when she was done with me.

I never did go to college. For one, I couldn't afford it. Rosalee had a small inheritance from her parents' death and took out some hardship loans that I never even considered applying for.

I just kept working and living, going through the motions of life and wishing I could turn the tables, turn back the clock for a little while…

Now, this weekend was an opportunity for me to

reconnect with my beloved cousin. Mara might be her best friend, but she didn't know Rosalee like I did. She didn't know her secrets. And she didn't know that this whole thing was a charade…

Rosalee would never be happy with Asher. There were too many things she kept hidden from him and no successful marriage starts out on a mountain of lies.

Chapter Five

GEORGIA

The groom's friend

Two people walk behind me, voices rising in a heated political debate. Masks and hats. Peace and war. Their voices grew angrier, as they sharpened their knives. Everyone thought they were right; unequivocally right. Perhaps we were all wrong for fighting.

I pushed myself through the double doors of the Louis Armstrong international airport, and was instantly assaulted by balmy air and bright yellow sunlight. I probably looked ridiculous in my jeans and long-sleeved T-shirt. My feet ached from my too-tight shoes.

Get me away from these people, this world, I thought. I couldn't stand being in public anymore. And it wasn't just the 'public' sphere either, it was everywhere—on my newsfeed, in my email inbox, on the TV screen and radio. I couldn't get away from it. Perhaps trying to get away from it was wrong—immoral. But I needed a break from the stress, to escape from my problems back home and the terror that came from everyday life in this modern world...

"Did you sleep on the plane? I was out like a light before we even hit the runway," Elizabeth said, cozying up beside me with her Hermes bag in the crook of her arm, her matching rolling case beside her. I'd barely noticed her walking with me, I'd been so eager to escape the loud voices of the plane and the keyed-up tourists in baggage claim.

"No. I wish I could have slept," I smiled. "I tried to read but couldn't. People were talking and the lights were so bright... plus I was too excited about this weekend." I added. A total lie. But over the years, I'd grown accustomed to lying to Asher's parents, as well as my own. Elizabeth Beake knew as much about me as I wanted her to—she saw the side of me that enjoyed people-pleasing, the strong side that kept my woes to myself...

"Well, at least that makes one of us," Elizabeth grumbled, turning back to look for her daughter Bri, as well as Mara and Rosalee.

Moments later, Rosalee came whooshing through the revolving doors of the airport with her shabby suitcase, followed by Bri and Mara with their massive cases and bags. I envied Rosalee in that moment. I wished I had packed light too; I could have saved some money on the luggage fees. God knows I needed to save money...

Bri and Mara had spent most of the flight in the center aisle, ignoring each other and buried in their phones. Rosalee had a window seat—courtesy of being the guest of honor, of course—but she'd left the shade down for the entire ride, leaning her head against the window, possibly sleeping.

Mara had already called for our ride after landing and she stepped forward, curly blond waves bouncing, and held up her hand at a peachy orange Focus.

The driver was friendly and popped out of his seat, running around the cheesy, bright vehicle to collect our bags. Elizabeth and Bri, mother and daughter, slid into the backseat together. *First at everything as usual.* Mara glanced at me, raising her eyebrows. It couldn't be more obvious that she didn't like me. She certainly didn't trust me... perhaps because she was Rosalee's best friend, and she didn't trust my role in Asher's life.

"Go ahead, Rosalee," I said, ushering the bride-to-be into the car next to her future sister-in-law, despite Bri's flicker of irritation.

The Beakes' were comfortable with me, they knew me. So, I could understand why they gravitated toward me instead of Asher's future wife, Rosalee. But I didn't want them hanging all over me this weekend. It was important for Rosalee to trust me since I was her future husband's best friend, after all.

"Oh. Thanks." Rosalee looked lost, still clutching her suitcase even though the others had loaded theirs into the trunk.

"I'll take the front." I jumped into the cab before Mara could stop me, leaving her to squeeze in as fourth in the back.

As soon as we were off, the driver was talking— chatting with a working-class, New Orleans Yat accent, the low O's and A's reminding me vaguely of my time in Boston. I did my best to tune them out, rolling down my window for air then digging through my handbag for my cell phone.

I had turned my phone off deliberately while paying for long-term parking at the airport. My friends had encouraged me not to leave my expensive Beemer in the long-term lot at the airport, but with the way things had been going in my life, I couldn't care less about seeing my car or returning to my old life again.

Although this weekend getaway was meant to be temporary, there were many reasons for me to avoid going home.

My hands were trembling as I slid the phone out, leaning my body toward the window to get some privacy. I pressed the on button and waited, watching as the Apple symbol appeared and my home screen bloomed into view.

No beeps, no ringing. *Maybe if I'm lucky*, I thought...

But then my phone came to life like the half-dead villain in a horror movie, one sharp ding followed by another.

"My, my! Someone's awfully popular," Elizabeth teased from the backseat. I pretended I couldn't hear over the rushing wind flowing in from my window.

"Probably her yoga clients wondering when she's coming back," Bri said, quietly. I couldn't help but roll my eyes. *Yeah, my yoga clients. All five of them.*

"Or all her loving Instagram followers," Mara chirped. I noticed the sarcasm dripping from her voice but chose to ignore it. I had bigger things to worry about than Rosalee's bulldog of a best friend.

Since leaving the nursing field and opening my own fitness studio, I'd failed miserably at building my client list, and I was struggling to keep the lights on and water running in my corner-lot building with its slow, non-existent daytime traffic. The yoga studio was an epic failure, by any measure. Sure, I had lots of Instagram and Twitter followers who liked my fitness posts and seemingly random selfies, but that didn't always compute into actual interest in my yoga classes. There were companies that offered me free products sometimes, but products don't pay the bills...

There were ten messages waiting in my text app. I clicked on the first one, tucking the phone close to my chest and toward the window, and scanned the words. They were written in all caps.

YOU CAN RUN BUT YOU CAN'T HIDE BITCH.

And the second one:

I KNOW WHERE YOU WENT AND I'M COMING.

Someone touched my shoulder. I jumped, juggling the phone until eventually, it fell to the floor. I whipped my head around. It was Rosalee, leaning over my shoulder. Had she seen the messages? My chest clenched with fear.

"Have you been to New Orleans before?" she asked sweetly, voice soft as a mouse.

I sighed. Hopefully she didn't see anything. She was just being friendly, and I should do the same. After all, the whole point of this trip was to celebrate her marriage to my best friend…

"No, I haven't. Have you?" I forced a smile, swallowing back the dread and fear in my chest, trying to disconnect the shaky fear in my chest from my voice. *I'm coming*, those words ran like a scroll in my brain. *I know where you went…*

Rosalee shook her head and sat back in her seat, looking scrunched and uncomfortable between Bri and Mara. I had to admit, Rosalee was a hard one to figure out. She seemed sweet and friendly, and I knew Asher was crazy about her. That was why he proposed. But I often got the sense that she didn't like me or trust me, and I wondered what she really thought of my friendship with Asher. I didn't blame her. If my fiancé was hanging around with another woman, I'd be skeptical too…

"Look!" Bri pointed from the backseat. We were approaching the square, traffic moving slow. A group of children stood on the corner under a bright green awning, shirtless with big wide smiles as they played their songs. A trombone slid forward and back, one kid sat on his haunches beating a hand drum while others strummed guitars. It was a joyous sound, buzzing and vibrant, and the kids were drawing a crowd. It was the kind of moment that should have made me feel happy and excited, but the adrenaline swooshing through my veins from those texts had caused a different type of rush.

As the others were watching the bands and crowds from the back windows, I ducked down to scoop up my phone from the floor. I didn't read the other eight messages—there would be time for that later. And let's face it, the messages would be the same. Threatening and angry. The sender wanted me dead, simple as that. They couldn't have made their point any clearer...

I opened a new message and typed quickly, reaching out to the only living soul who understood my concerns and could provide some sort of solace.

Asher, I'm scared. I wish you were here. I don't feel safe anywhere right now.

Chapter Six

ROSALEE

The bride-to-be

There was a roaring in my eyes, my tongue stuck to the roof of my mouth, and my head was pounding as we arrived at the Leblanc-Landry house for my bachelorette party.

Bachelorette party. What a joke.

How was I supposed to get married to the man of my dreams when I knew something was going on between him and Georgia?

I couldn't see what she was texting, but I saw his name. Georgia communicated more with my own future-husband than I did…

I'd checked my messages when I got off the plane. Not a single one from Asher.

Furthermore, why had I found a recurring charge for her yoga gym on our bank statements?!

I'd spent most of the flight pretending to sleep as I scrolled through our online joint bank account, ignoring the airline's rules about putting my phone in airplane mode. The charges began last August, right after she opened the gym. It had been so long since I'd checked our account, trusting Asher to manage our finances. The fact that I hadn't looked through our banking info sooner made me feel sheepish and naive...

What if I am about to marry a man who is unfaithful? Asher, who loathed exercise and rarely had time for sleeping, much less working out for leisure by doing stupid yoga...

I wondered how many nights or weekends he pretended to be working late or going in to finish paperwork on a case, when really, he was visiting the yoga studio with Georgia on a regular basis.

My mind was reeling with images of Georgia, her tawny, lithe body in its sports bras and Lycra shorts, stretching and bending, shaping her body in ways I never could, to please him...

There was a gasp beside me. "Oh my gosh, isn't it gorgeous?! Please tell me you love it, Rosie-Poo!" Mara squealed.

I hadn't heard my best friend call me that ridiculous

nickname—Rosie-Poo—since freshman year of college. I stared at her, blinked, then looked up at the house.

I felt an almost out-of-body sensation, a strange detachment from reality. I could barely remember the ride here, my mind and body so preoccupied with my boyfriend's possible—*probable*—affair with Georgia.

But now, seeing my best friend's face lit up like a Christmas tree—cheeks wide and strained, waiting and praying for a good reaction from me—I couldn't help feeling ashamed.

Asher be damned. I was here with my friends. Mara and Tinsley had gone to a whole lot of trouble—not to mention expense! —to celebrate this moment with me. Despite everything, I owed them my pleasure and grace this weekend…

Mara and I were the first to emerge from the car; the house loomed larger than life before me, taking my breath away.

"I don't know what to say. This place is… It's so breathtaking, Mara. I can't believe I'm really here. It's like something out of a storybook!" I grabbed her into a hug, feeling the sting of tears as I held her. "Thank you for doing this. You and Tinsley…" I whispered into her hair.

The house truly was like a storybook mansion. Marble columns and ivy. Wrought-iron balconies and licks of dark green crawling up the sides of it.

71

There was even a large bride and groom—either plastic characters or inflatables, I couldn't tell which. And brilliant décor stretched all the way over the front of the house, like a great big birthday present just for me.

"You deserve it. This weekend is all about you. And your marriage to Asher, of course," Mara said.

I looked around at the others, who were gathering their bags from the trunk. I watched Elizabeth slip the driver a five-dollar bill. *Cheapskate.*

But even she looked impressed as she turned toward the house, eyes crawling up the columns and beams, taking it all in.

This place truly is magnificent, I thought.

"I can't wait to see what the inside looks like," Georgia said, shimmying up beside me, graceful as a gazelle. She slipped an arm around my shoulders, and instantly my whole body tensed. I didn't trust her. Never had. And now I knew why... Asher had been attending her gym regularly, spending time alone with her, since last August. If it was simply platonic, why didn't he invite me along, or at the very least, tell me about it?!

Beyond the house, the sun was just starting to fall below the horizon.

"I hope Tinsley's here, but I didn't see her car." And just like that, as though she could hear my words—as she had always been able to, in that psychic way of hers, since we were kids— Tinsley's face appeared at a window on the second level.

She was ghostly pale, long white-blond hair draped around her gaunt face like wispy drapes. She wasn't smiling. One palm was flattened against the glass, and she was staring straight at me. I waved at my cousin, relieved to see her. When Mara had made that dramatic statement in the airport bathroom about her not coming, I'd been crushed. But then, learning she was driving instead, I felt less annoyed. *At least she's here*, I thought. That was all that mattered.

"Jesus, look at that ghoul. Are we sure that's a real-life person? Perhaps this place is haunted?" Elizabeth sniffed from behind me, following my gaze to the shape of Tinsley in the window.

I whipped my head around and bared my teeth at her, forgetting for a moment that I was supposed to be kind and courteous to my future husband's mom. My possibly *cheating* future husband...

"That's my cousin, Tinsley, and she's beautiful," I said, sharply.

Elizabeth gave me a startled look, as though she were seeing me for the first time.

"Tinsley is the other half of the planning committee," Mara sang, ushering all of us forward with a painted-on smile. "She decided to drive up early instead of flying; I told Rosalee, but I guess I forgot to mention it to the rest of you."

Before anyone could say more, the door to the Leblanc-Landry mansion creaked open, allowing us to enter. There was no one waiting on the other side.

Chapter Seven

BRI

The sister-in-law

The house was stunning, with its classic and otherworldly design and its dark gothic interior. Honestly, I was impressed by all of it—Rosalee's friend, Mara, had great taste, and had proven to be more outgoing and headstrong than my soon-to-be sister-in-law.

Even Mom looked impressed, and she had been decidedly tight-lipped since her faux pas at arrival, making fun of Rosalee's ghoulish cousin in the window. In Mom's defense, Tinsley did look like a ghost up there —like that creepy Carol Anne girl from *Poltergeist*, with her blank face and hand so desperately pressed to the glass...

Locking the door to my own personal bedroom suite, I was relieved to finally be away from the others, if only for a short while. *Dinner will be served at seven,* the hostess Delfina had announced within moments of our arrival, like a creepy, robotic butler from the Victorian ages.

I had just under half an hour to unpack, unwind, and mentally prepare myself for the weekend ahead.

As much as the house intrigued me, I was itching to get away from it, to find my way to Bourbon Street and order a mixed cocktail or two.

For now, I settled on a glass of water from the ensuite bathroom. Then I splashed my face and rubbed my eyes with a fluffy white towel. Looking at my own reflection in the dull yellow light of the vanity mirror, I could barely recognize myself. But that's how it always was these days—twenty-one became twenty-five, and the next thing I knew I was celebrating my thirty-fifth birthday.

My eyes were puffy from the flight, and from lack of sleep the night before. My shoulders were stiff—stiffer than usual. The twist of my mouth I recognized from when I was desperate for a drink, or I needed my medication.

Back in the bedroom, I unloaded my suitcase, grateful when I found my prescription bottle for my anti-anxiety meds. I popped one, then popped an extra, swallowing the pills whole without water. Although I knew they took a while to take effect, the results *felt* immediate—my shoulders relaxed, and it seemed like I could breathe a little more easily. The last thing I needed was a drink; my doctor had warned me that mixing pills and alcohol was dangerous and potentially fatal. But, surely, a couple pills and a few glasses of wine never killed nobody…

Finally, I was able to look around and take in the grandness of my room. I wondered if the others' rooms were as palatial as mine—hopefully not *better* than mine, I thought, uneasily.

The four-poster bed was draped with a silky, white duvet and sprinkled with tiny flowers—yellow and white daisies. A thick, lush robe with my name embroidered on the breast was laid out in the center. Impulsively, I stripped out of my too-tight khakis and top, kicked off my shoes, and wrapped the creamy robe around me, tightening the belt. It fit perfectly.

Speaking of fits, I couldn't help feeling bad about Rosalee's T-shirt. I'd wanted to please Mom when I chose a shirt two sizes too small, but truthfully, I'd just made a fool of myself. Mara had come equipped with her own back-up shirts for everyone, and they were much more tasteful and well-fitted than mine.

But Rosalee knew what me and my mother were like, and if she planned on joining this family, then she'd better get used to the judgy stares and passive-aggressiveness that came with it…

I agreed with Mom. Rosalee wasn't good enough for my brother, and there was something shady and flaky about her. But Mom's fixation on her weight bothered me. Part of me got a good laugh out of Mom's petty present at Christmas. But the other part... the other part felt ashamed and insulted by it. After all, I had never been slim and fit like my mother either; I was built like a bull just like my father.

But ever since Dad died a few years ago, Mom had become a complete mess. She might not have let it show to strangers, or to my baby brother, but I could see it— she was lost without Dad. She had no one to take care of or bicker with. No one to keep her company at night. If focusing all her energy on criticizing Rosalee kept her mind off her grief over Dad, then so be it. It was just a little harmless teasing.

From my bedroom window, I had a brilliant view of a bricked-in courtyard. It sparkled with string lights, little iron tables and chairs scattered around like a café in Paris. And below my balcony, I could see the eerie shimmer of an inground swimming pool. Perfect. All I needed was a stiff drink and a lounge chair, and I'd be good to go...

There was a sharp rap on my door, making me jump.

"Dinner in five minutes!" Mara shouted; her mouth sounded like it was pressed right up against the door.

"Okay," I grumbled. Where had the time gone?

I threw off the robe, struggled into a new outfit, and added a spot of peach blush to my cheeks. I always tried to look and act more feminine around Mom. I knew she wanted a daughter more like Georgia: pretty and lithe, sociable and distinctly girlish. But that wasn't me. As much as I would like for it to be, it wasn't.

I finger-combed my hair and was just about to head out the door for dinner when my cell phone chimed in my bag. I was so ravenous, I almost considered leaving it for later, but I always had to be available for work, being the only one capable of keeping systems online or rerouting servers when they went down.

I dug the phone out of my bag and clicked on the message.

I'm so pissed off; I could kill her!

Sighing, I sent back a quick reply:

You and me both.

Chapter Eight

ROSALEE

The bride-to-be

I followed the rich, smoky smells of food down the double-sided staircase of the Leblanc-Landry mansion. I'd packed away my T-shirt from Mara—as much as I appreciated the gesture, I wanted to wear my own clothes now that we were here. I'd pawed through my miniature suitcase, finding the perfect dinner dress: a comfy, cotton sundress that was slightly wrinkled from travel and my recent move, but fit snug on my hips and breasts, accentuating the best parts of my curvy figure.

The others were waiting as I descended the stairs, and I couldn't help feeling like a blushing bride already. Was this how it would feel on my wedding day? All eyes on me, watchful and engaged?

"I don't know what's cooking, but it smells delicious! I don't deserve all this, guys."

"Oh, but you do," Mara said, taking me by the elbow and leading me down a low-lit corridor toward an enormous, grand dining space. Tinsley followed at my heels; I'd had only a few moments to speak with my cousin upon arriving, and I wanted a chance to get her alone so we could catch up like old times.

As much as it hurt thinking about the past, Tinsley was a huge part of mine—an important part that I couldn't just swallow down and cast aside. We had stayed in touch over the last several years, through college and apartments, through life, but it was different seeing her face to face again. Although my hometown was less than ninety miles from Moon County, we had somehow avoided seeing each other for years. There were always excuses, mostly on my end, work and appointments, too much going on with planning the wedding to have a proper sit down and catch-up with my dear cousin.

"My god!" Elizabeth exclaimed from behind me as we entered the room. She pointed at the huge spread of food—the biggest feast I'd ever seen. "We could feed an entire town of people with all this food," she said, her lips curled with obvious disapproval.

"Well, if you'd like, Miss Beake, we could gather up the leftovers when we're done and take them down to the homeless shelter or encampments. There are plenty of homeless in New Orleans you could meet," Mara said. "Wouldn't that be something nice to share for your Facebook followers?" Mara was still going.

I cringed at the exchange. Elizabeth Beake wouldn't be caught dead helping the homeless. And if she did, Mara was right—she'd surely post about it on Facebook to make herself and her daughter and of course, Saint Georgia, look good. Always with the holier-than-thou routine...

I sidled up next to Tinsley and smiled, brushing her forearm with the tips of my fingers like we did when we were kids.

"Isn't it marvelous?" I breathed, nodding at the gorgeous spread.

"Sure is," Tinsley said, quietly. She muttered something else under her breath that sounded like, "Looks expensive."

"Thank you for helping plan the party. I know Mara can be a bit..." I couldn't think of the right word to describe my best friend from college. 'Bossy' wasn't enough to cover it. Mara could be downright intimidating and mean when she wanted to be, and Tinsley, with her quiet and introverted disposition, was quite the opposite.

"No problem," Tinsley said, turning to get a good look at me for the first time. She smiled, showing all her teeth. It had been so long since I'd seen her smile, and I'd forgotten how beautiful and ethereal she truly was. *Like the Sugar Plum Fairy in the Nutcracker,* I used to tell her when we were kids. But she looked so much older now, and thinner too. The baby fat of youth was gone, bones stretching over her skin, collarbones sharp like daggers poking through her chest. God, how I'd missed her though. I wondered if she'd missed me too...

"Come on, my beautiful bride! Your place is right here at the head of the table!" Mara ushered me away from my cousin, pulling out a heavy, high-backed chair with a screech, and all but pushing me into my seat.

"Thank you," I sputtered, adjusting my chair and locating my fancy white dinner napkin on my plate. I placed it on my lap as I watched the others. Elizabeth and Bri took seats farther down the table, as far away from me as possible. Tinsley came around and took the chair to my right, and before Mara could sweep in and join my left, Georgia plopped down beside me.

"I'm famished. Can you believe all this food?" Georgia sighed, opening her napkin with a flicker of flare.

"It's... a lot," I said, eyes roaming all the way down to the end of the table, trying to take in the enormous spread. It was beautiful, its own piece of artwork, really. Just looking at it made me want to paint, perhaps with oils...

The colors and shapes, the heaping bowls and platters of food in their fancy, bone-white china. Some of the food was what I considered classic New Orleans cuisine, most of which I'd never tried—several types of gumbo, which smelled spicy and delicious, heaps of blood-red crawfish, tails and eyes and all, with sausage and corn, the biggest crab legs I'd ever seen, red beans and rice, jambalaya, and a few different mystery soups. As though that weren't enough, I spotted fried fish and chicken, and several different types of potatoes.

My mouth watered as my eyes roved from dish to dish, wondering how I would reach it all from my place at the head of the table. But part of me had to agree with Elizabeth, which came as a shock to me. This was too much food. Even for six hungry grown women.

Mara was standing in front of her seat, phone in hand, trying to get the perfect picture. Finally, I watched her stand up on the seat of her fancy chair and snap a full photo of the food spread from above. When she was done, she turned toward me and smiled, pointing her phone's camera at my face and clicking over and over. Great. More double-chinned photos for Facebook, Twitter, and Instagram.

The head of staff, or so I presumed, emerged from the kitchen with two other waiters. Her name was Delfina, if I remembered correctly. She looked old and matronly, and serious in her stiff, white apron.

Each waiter carried several bottles of alcohol, elegantly holding each one as though it were a treasured gift.

Delfina arrived at my right elbow and smiled politely. "Welcome to our guest of honor. What would you like to start with? Champagne, or wine? I have red and white."

I'd never been much of a wine drinker, preferring soda or tea with my meals. Asher liked to drink beer occasionally, and sometimes I drank a bottle or two with him when he got home from work. But wine wasn't really my thing.

But tonight was all about me. *It's a celebration*, I reminded myself. It was okay to cut loose, and maybe alcohol would help me shake off this nervous edge I couldn't help feeling. Plus, turning it down felt rude. They talked about peer pressure like it was something that only affected teens, but adulthood was just as bad, or worse, sometimes.

"I'll try the champagne, please."

Delfina poured a small amount in my shiny glass and then nodded expectantly, waiting for me to taste it.

"Oh." I lifted the glass to my lips, sniffing the bubbly mist rising off the top of it. I took a sip, jaw locking a bit from the sour flinch of it.

"It's perfect," I lied. "Thank you."

As the wait staff moved around the table, filling each woman's glass, we passed around the heavy dishes of food. I was so hungry, and it all looked good, so I added a bit of everything to my plate as it came around. *This is like a Cajun Thanksgiving,* I thought, taking a few large gulps of champagne. The more I tried the fizzy drink, the more the sourness dissipated.

Elizabeth, down at the end of the table, was being picky with her choices—passing completely on some things with a disdainful look and scooping tiny portions onto her plate of others. She had passed on the alcohol too, requesting bottled water instead. *Evian, if you have it,* I heard her murmur to one of the waiters.

Bri, on the other hand, had already downed her glass of red, and lifted her glass for a second round before they had finished pouring drinks for the other guests.

"So, you decided to drive, huh? How was the trip down?" I asked Tinsley, trying a bit of the sausage gumbo. I closed my eyes, taking in the smoky richness of it. It was one of the best things I'd ever tasted. Or perhaps I was just that hungry.

"Yeah, you know how I am with crowds. And I'm not too fond of planes these days, either. The drive was beautiful though. It reminded me of the old days when we used to ride around in Mom's hatchback, smoking cigarettes and listening to her Alanis Morrissette's cassettes on repeat. Remember that?"

I did. Windows down, smoke rolling out in waves. The two us, belting out the angry girl lyrics in unison.

"Those were the days," I said, softly, reaching for one of the crawdads. It looked interesting, but I wasn't quite sure how to eat it.

"Like this," Georgia said, touching my elbow. I flinched. For some reason, being near her right now was making my flesh crawl. Surely, if she and Asher were sleeping together, she wouldn't have agreed to be my bridesmaid, would she? She wouldn't keep up this whole charade of being the dutiful and supportive friend unless she was just that evil. Some women were...

Georgia lifted a crawdad in front of her face and twisted the head with a snap. I watched in horror as she tossed the head aside and peeled back the shell. *Ew.* Next, she slid the meat out of the shell and dropped it in her mouth with a big, fleshy smile.

"Delish," she said, mouth full of food.

It probably was delicious, but I'd lost my appetite. This girl even made eating crustaceans look sexy. Ugh.

"So, how's the yoga business going, Georgia?" My voice sounded different—too loud, the words curling off my tongue too fast. Everything was getting blurry around the edges of my world, feeling less real. Less consequential. Somehow, when I looked down at my flute, I realized one of the waiters had filled it again.

"So, the yoga...?" I slurred between gulps of the champagne. I put a finger up, mimicking Bri from earlier, and one of the waiters rushed over to fill my glass.

Georgia finished chewing. "Yoga is going well. I love it, truly. But you know how it is with your own business… It takes a while to get things off the ground."

"Not really," I shrugged. My art was never my *business*. Sure, I'd made a few hundred bucks off my paintings here and there, volunteered to do lessons for kids' parties, school events, or the like. But being an artist, for me, had never been very profitable. Most of my income came from my side jobs: cleaning houses and businesses and, keeping accounts for my local church.

"I've been meaning to stop by the studio. Do you have some sort of sign-up for it? A monthly pass?" I belched, my stomach roiling with bubbles. *In other words, is my soon-to-be husband one of your monthly regulars? Sneaking around, spending time one-on-one at your fancy pants stupid studio?*

"No, not yet. I don't have enough clients for that," Georgia said, quietly.

Liar! I was tempted to call her out on it, right then and there. And why not? What did I have to lose, really?

But as I polished off my third glass of champagne, head buzzing from the alcohol, I reminded myself that I had a lot to lose: the man of my dreams, the dreamboat wedding, the chance for real happiness…

Georgia was quiet now, eyes focused on her plate, pushing around her beans and rice with the tines of her fork.

From the corner of my eye, I could feel Tinsley watching me. That mother hen concern of hers—even though we were the same age, she had always been the quiet one. The reasonable and responsible one. The smart one.

I shot her a tight smile. "This food is divine," I said, lifting my glass with a careless splash, and looking down the table at Mara, too. Mara was stuck sitting across from Bri and Elizabeth, who appeared to be in their own little cocoon, talking amongst themselves. *Probably planning their next mean stunt for Christmas*, I thought, angrily.

But no, that wasn't right. *Elizabeth looks annoyed with Bri*, I realized, squinting through my droopy eyes and double vision. I'd seen Elizabeth agitated before, getting that judgy look in her eyes many times since making her acquaintance. But I'd never seen that look directed at her own daughter.

Bri was gulping large mouthfuls of wine now; her lips and teeth were stained dark purple, like congealed blood. She gave me a wolfish smile when she caught me looking at them and tilted the bottle back to her lips once more. I'd never seen Bri drunk before. Although she had consumed several glasses, she seemed tipsier than the rest of us. *Under the influence of something else, perhaps?* I wondered, my thoughts turning sluggish and overly introspective.

"Thank you so much for planning this," I shouted

down the table at Mara. "And you, too, of course." I lifted my glass in Tinsley's direction.

"Oh, just you wait until you see the desserts they're bringing out!" Mara squealed. "I got all your favorites, plus some New Orleans delicacies..." She lifted her wine glass at me, then grinned.

I glanced over at Tinsley again, but she was watching Mara. Something passed between the two of them, something I hadn't seen before. Gosh. What was everyone's deal tonight? I had a right to be pissed off—my fiancé might be sleeping with Georgia, the stretchy-legged temptress, but why was everyone else on edge with each other?

Right on cue, Delfina and her helpers emerged from the shadows, as though they had been there all along, simply part of the woodwork and wallpaper design.

"If it's all right with you, I'm going to clear some space for the desserts now," Delfina said, directing her question first to Mara, then to me.

"Sounds great," I said. Although the champagne had tasted okay, a flash of heartburn was already eroding my chest and esophagus. One of the waiters came to fill my glass for a fourth time, but I covered the top and shook my head. I was buzzed enough; I didn't want to do or say anything to make a fool out of myself or ruin my own party. After all, my friends had gone to so much trouble for me already...

Platters of fish and potatoes were whisked away, jambalaya and soups scooted over for yet more food. *All of this food, destined for the garbage probably*, I realized. There was so much left uneaten.

I watched as the waiters laid out silver trays and lifted the lids one by one.

"Don't forget about..." Mara said, glancing over her shoulder at Delfina.

"It's right here, Miss." Delfina carried a large white plate with a gorgeous slab of tiramisu in the center of it. Mara had actually chosen my favorite dessert, tiramisu; my mother used to make it for me when she was alive. I hadn't realized Mara knew that; perhaps Tinsley was the one who told her and picked out the dessert.

"Here you are." Delfina set the dessert plate in front of me and stepped back, tucking her hands primly behind her. The dessert looked wonderful, fancy shavings and flakes of chocolate dotted around the plate like artwork. Almost too pretty to eat.

One of the waiters arrived, placing a tiny bowl of whipped cream beside my plate.

"Thank you," I said, breathing in the heavenly smells of cocoa and cream.

"And not just that! You have to try all these, too!" Mara exclaimed. She was scooping dessert for herself onto a clean plate. I spotted ice cream and a bright lemon cake, and a colored ring cake that showed off the traditional colors of New Orleans: purple, green, and gold.

Even Bri and Elizabeth were keen, reaching for their own sweet helpings with spoons.

"Wait a second. That's not a king cake, is it?" Tinsley gasped, leaning up on her elbows to see the colorful ringed dessert in the middle.

"As a matter of fact, it is!" Mara said, ripping it apart to get a piece. "These are a staple of New Orleans, and if it's made right, there might even be a little plastic baby inside. Baby Jesus..."

"No, no, no. It's not baby Jesus. And you're not supposed to eat king cake after Fat Tuesday!" Tinsley exclaimed.

Her face was so serious, eyes hard and round with fear. I placed a hand over my mouth, suddenly feeling drunk again as I tried to stifle a giggle. All of these little squabbles seemed ridiculous now that I wasn't sober.

"And why ever not?" Elizabeth said, forkful of colorful cake poised in the air by her perfectly lined lips.

"It's very bad luck to eat king cake now; it's only for carnival season. The people in New Orleans are superstitious about this. We can't eat it," Tinsley warned.

I stared at her face, trying to determine if she was being serious. She certainly looked serious to me.

Mara snorted with laughter. "I'm guessing you read that in one of your books! This isn't the 1900s, Tinsley!

It's okay to eat the cake. Go on, everyone. Try it! It wasn't cheap," Mara said, filling her mouth and raising her brows in triumph at Tinsley.

"Jesus. Like you would know." Tinsley dropped her fork, rattling her plate, and pushed back her chair.

Something was going on between her and Mara, something more than a silly cake.

"Well, I for one am not superstitious. I believe in making my own luck," Bri slurred, reaching for the platter of cake and pulling it toward her.

"Me too," Georgia said, giving Tinsley an apologetic smile as she stood and made her way to the end of the table to reach the desserts more easily. She began filling her plate with an assortment of desserts.

Delfina was back, carrying a small gold basket in her hands.

Holy hell. Please not more desserts, I'm about to burst, I thought, miserably.

"These are for you, ma'am. To read aloud, or for after the dinner." She set the basket down beside my barely touched tiramisu and stepped away.

The basket contained tiny white pieces of paper notes, which were folded into neat, little squares.

"What is this?" I asked, looking from Tinsley to Mara.

"Those are your well wishes! We all wrote them for you. You know how women do them at baby showers? Like, advice for new moms and shit? I thought we could all give you some new marriage advice, or well wishes for your future marriage," Mara explained. Her words were slurred now, too; she lifted her wine again, taking a deep sip.

"Oh wow. This is so sweet," I said, slowly rotating the basket. "And the basket itself is lovely, too. What a thoughtful idea. Thank you." I'd been smiling so much and saying thank you so often, that my mouth and cheeks felt numb.

The food and champagne rumbled in my belly, and I fought back the urge to excuse myself and go lie down.

"Should I read them now, then?" I looked over at Tinsley. She was leaning back in her chair, ghostly white and arms crossed. *Wow. She really is pissed off about that cake tradition,* I realized.

Tinsley shrugged.

"Yes, but only if you want to," Mara said. But I could tell she wanted me to; she was sitting on the edge of her seat, elbows on the table, centimeters away from taking a dip in whipping cream.

"Yes, read them!" Bri bellowed, then she let out a long, low burp that startled her mother beside her.

"Bri Michaela, excuse you," Elizabeth snapped. For the first time ever, Elizabeth looked truly disgusted with her drunken daughter.

I held back another giggle. Michaela was Bri's middle name, huh? I wondered how often her mother had used her middle name, or Asher's, when she scolded them as children.

I lifted the first note in the basket and carefully unfolded it. Despite the stress of my concerns over Asher and the mild tension at the table, I couldn't help feeling a small rush of joy. My friends, family, and soon-to-be in-laws had written kind notes for me. I was a lucky woman to have this many people celebrating my marriage to Asher...

The note was simple but sweet. I read the words aloud: "Never go to bed angry. Tell your spouse you love them, even when they're getting on your last damn nerve."

I looked up and smiled, then folded the note back and set it aside.

"Thank you," I said, for the millionth time. "But I don't know who wrote it. Are they all anonymous?" I looked around the table, searching their eyes, wondering who wrote that one. *Maybe Mara or Georgia*, I thought. It seemed too nice to be from Elizabeth or Bri.

Speaking of Georgia, she barely seemed to be paying attention. She was bolting down a large helping of lemon pie, a spot of cream on her nose. I'd never seen her eat so much. One had to wonder how she maintained such a good figure, even with all that yoga she did.

The next note was another short one. Before I could

read it aloud, my eyes were scanning the single sentence, absorbing the words on the tiny card.

KEEP HIM SEXUALLY SATISFIED SO I DON'T HAVE TO ANYMORE.

There was a blinding flash; Mara snapping more photos for social media.

I let out a small gasp, and quickly reached for the next.

The second note wasn't as jarring as the first, but it still sent a shockwave through me.

I KNOW ALL OF YOUR SECRETS AND SOON YOUR HUSBAND WILL TOO.

"What is it? What do they say?" Elizabeth asked, hawklike and smiling from the other end of the table.

"Nothing. Just more sage advice. Thank you all so much. I hate to be a party pooper, but I think I ate too much. Is it okay if I go and lie down for a bit?"

I didn't wait for an answer as I scooped up my basket of 'well wishes' and pushed my chair back which resulted in a loud screech on the old, wood floors.

"Of course. It's been a long day," Tinsley said, touching my elbow. I felt a flicker of something—

recognition and safety; she was one of the few people in this world I could trust and that truly knew me.

I glanced once more at Elizabeth. She was watching me, eyes calculating. Did she write that to stir up drama … or could it really have been from Georgia?

As I tucked my chair in, I looked over at Georgia, searching for a hint that she wrote one of those awful, mean sentences.

But something else was going on with Georgia. Her face was beet-red, her eyes dark black holes in her head. She had her hands up near her throat area, fingers fluttering with panic.

"Georgia?" I placed a hand on her shoulder, but she jerked away from me, coughing and sputtering so hard that I had to grab the back of her chair to keep it from falling to the ground.

"What is it? What's wrong?" Delfina and the waiters rushed to Georgia's side, shared looks of alarm on their faces.

Georgia was gasping for air. She pointed at the cake. "Did that have coconut in it?" she croaked each word painfully between rasping breaths.

Delfina's eyes grew wide as quarters. "Oh no, are you allergic?"

But before she could say any more, Georgia had slithered out of her chair and onto the floor, lungs whistling as she struggled to take in air.

I looked over at Tinsley and Bri, panic fluttering through my chest. Oh my god, someone had to do something!

"Call 911, Tinsley! Please!" I shouted while kneeling down beside Georgia on the floor. I'd taken a first aid course as a teenager, but I had no idea what to do, everything I'd learned was now a hazy memory after the alcohol I'd consumed.

Tinsley was out of her seat, struggling to find her phone in her pocket. I stared at Georgia, wide-eyed, as she struggled for air, a strange mixture of emotions running through me.

"What's the address here again?" Tinsley shouted. One of the waiters moved to her side and took the phone, shouting clear instructions to the operator on the other end of the line.

Elizabeth and Bri were now on the floor beside us. Elizabeth was on her knees with her face close to Georgia's, cooing like a small child and rubbing soothing circles on her back. "It's going to be okay, just breathe very slowly. Help is on the way, I promise."

The only person not standing over Georgia with a look of concern was Mara. When I looked up at her, I saw that she was smirking, a look of unmistakable glee in her eyes.

Chapter Nine

MARA

The best friend

They blamed me. Of course, they did, and truth be told, they had every right to be angry. Because I blamed myself too...

I knew she was allergic to coconut, okay? But I didn't ask for THIS.

I assumed Georgia would get splotchy, maybe a little itchy and uncomfortable, the way I did when I took antibiotics. I didn't realize she was *that* allergic. If she was, why didn't she carry some sort of EpiPen on her?!

We stood on the front lawn of the mansion, sirens loud and lights flashing, and watched as they loaded Georgia into the back of an ambulance.

"Do you think she'll be okay?" I said, turning to Tinsley.

"How the hell would I know?" she hissed. And then, "How could you overlook this, Mara? We asked everyone about their allergies months before you planned that ridiculous menu. We both knew Georgia was allergic to coconut!"

Rosalee was watching us, face blank. There was nothing behind the eyes; I couldn't tell if she was angry with me, worried for Georgia, or secretly pleased that her fiancé's female 'best friend' was being carted off to the ER.

"Well, maybe if I'd had more help with the planning, I would have made fewer mistakes!" I cried.

"Oh, okay! That's why it happened," Tinsley said, with wild laughter. "Blame the one person who's footing the bill for this whole thing. Doing the planning was the least you could do, Mara."

I gasped. How dare she? I'd told her I would pay her back, and I will. I just need to sort out a few things and figure out my bank account…

"I'm going with her. Someone needs to stay by Georgia's side," Elizabeth said, thankfully interrupting my exchange with Tinsley. We all watched as Elizabeth rushed off, hurrying to follow the EMS workers as they all hastily bundled into the ambulance.

From here, I could see Georgia lying flat on the

stretcher with an oxygen mask covering half her face. What the hell had I been thinking? She'd be okay ... right?!

"Mom..." Bri held an outstretched arm toward Elizabeth. She looked strangely desperate and childlike lying there, clumsy drunken fingers reaching for her mother.

Then she looked over at me, dropped her arm to her side, and burped. Wow. I didn't have 'blubbering alcoholic' on Bri's bingo card, but there was always room for surprises.

"I didn't know she was allergic," I lied, looking back and forth from Tinsley to Rosalee, then over to Bri. "There must have been some sort of mistake, something overlooked..."

"You can say that again," Tinsley snapped.

As the ambulance peeled away, sirens flickering in the dark, I turned toward the staff standing steely on the front porch. They had dropped the whole service act; one of the waiters was crying and another was comforting her. Delfina was the only one who seemed to be holding it together.

When she caught my eye, she shook her head from side to side. "I didn't know she was allergic. No one told me. If we had known about the allergy, I never would have served that lemon and coconut cake."

"It's not your fault," I said. "It's mine. Let's go inside.

I'll help you clean up and discuss the menu for tomorrow." I bounded up the steps, eager to get away from Tinsley and Rosalee's accusatory looks.

Once inside, I led Delfina and the waiters back down the long, dark hallway once again.

"It's not your fault," I repeated. "The meal was lovely. I didn't know about the allergy either, but I am totally to blame. I'm sure that Georgia will be just fine. They'll probably give her some steroids or epinephrine, and she'll back to as good as new by morning."

"I hope so," Delfina said, a touch of anger in her voice as she moved to clear away the remnants of our long-forgotten feast. She started gathering up the dishes, one by one, loading them into the crook of her arm.

"Go get the others," she snapped at one of the waiters who was standing in the wings, looking lost and distraught.

I started helping by carrying plates and bowls back to the kitchen. On one plate, a generous helping of king cake remained. It reminded me of Tinsley's stupid warning—the whole suspicious thing about eating the dessert outside of carnival season. She was so ridiculous and strange; I never did understand how Rosalee tolerated living with her for all those years.

But as I emerged into the dining room once again to gather more plates, I spotted the pair walking hand in hand up the stairs. Tinsley glanced over at me, once, narrowing her eyes as she shuffled Rosalee, stumbling and tipsy, up the stairs.

God, they were acting like I'd tried to kill Georgia. It was just a stupid mistake. She'd be fine. It was just a little allergy, right?

"Please, ma'am. Let me take it from here," said Delfina, nodding towards the rest of the food, scowling. Even she looked annoyed by my presence. "After we have cleaned up, the staff and I will leave for the night. I've put baguettes, cereals, and plenty of snacks in the cupboards and refrigerator for you all. .We will return tomorrow evening to drop off the bonfire supplies and the hors d'oeuvres you ordered," Delfina continued, scrubbing the table with too much force.

"Sounds great," I said, absently, turning back toward the stairs. The ghosts of Tinsley and Rosalee were long gone. Upstairs to bitch about me, no doubt.

But where has Bri gone off to? I wondered.

"If you need me before tomorrow evening, you have all my numbers, correct? And please keep me posted about Georgia," Delfina said, sternly. I could tell she was ready for me to leave her alone, let her finish the clean up without me hovering over her.

"I will."

The plan for tomorrow was a morning on the town, visiting Jackson Square and seeing the sights. Then I planned to surprise Rosalee and the others with a masseuse and makeup artist, to prepare for an exciting evening out, frolicking between bars on Bourbon Street. Then on our return, I'd planned a bonfire and appetizers for our final night before leaving on Sunday…

The perfect weekend. And now it had all gone to shit because of my own stupidity.

Because of my own impulsivity and selfishness.

A voice in my head said to me: *What if you killed her? What if she gets to the hospital and dies? How could you do something like that?*

But when it came to Rosalee, I was often over-protective and overzealous. I'd wanted this weekend to be perfect and instead of having a gaff at her arch nemesis, Georgia, I had taken it too far, and now the weekend was probably ruined. I just hoped Rosalee didn't think I'd done it on purpose. I was sure Tinsley knew, but as long as Rosalee still thought the best of me, that was all that mattered.

I bid goodnight to Delfina and the staff, then thanked them again for the extravagant meal. It had been a lovely spread—too costly and over-the-top and with a disastrous finale, but still lovely all the same.

I was about to head up the stairs myself, track down Rosalee and apologize a million times, but then I saw a flicker of light through the window. As I moved toward the glass, I saw a few more flickers in the dark.

I let myself out through the heavy glass doors and

was hit with a rush of balmy night air before I walked toward the low-lit courtyard.

Bri was leaning against the brick boundary between the courtyard and pool, trying to light a cigarette.

"Let me help." I leaned in, cupping my hands around hers to block out the breeze. As it caught light, I breathed in the sweet and mellow cloud of smoke from its tip.

"Don't tell my mom," Bri said, cigarette clenched between her teeth.

I rolled my eyes. "You're kidding, right? You must be like, what? Forty years old?"

"Thirty-five." Bri blew a puff of smoke in my face.

"Sorry."

"No need. I don't mind getting older. I mean, my mother minds it. She wanted me to be the one getting married, making babies and all that jazz ... but that's not the life for me." Bri shook her head and chuckled. "I'm not sure why I told you that."

"Because you're drunk. I think we all are a little bit."

"Not my mom. She hardly ever drinks now. She used to every night, a 'nightcap' she called it, until my father died. Now she avoids anything and everything that reminds her of him."

Despite all the drinking and burping, Bri didn't really seem all that drunk now. Her eyes and words were clear, and I could tell that talking about her late father was painful.

"Sorry about your dad," I said.

Despite the warm temperature, the breeze in the shadows of the courtyard felt chilly, goosebumps appearing on my arms and legs.

"Do you think Georgia will be okay?" I asked, staring over at the pool. The water looked crystal clear, as though the surface itself was an optical illusion.

"Oh yeah. She'll be okay. She had a few bouts with coconut when she was a kid. And Georgia is a nurse. If she thought her allergy was that bad, then she would have carried an EpiPen with her," Bri exhaled.

"A nurse? I thought she owned her own yoga studio?" I asked. Rosalee certainly hadn't mentioned anything about Georgia being a nurse, and her Instagram account was all fitness and sexy poses.

"Yeah. Something happened. I'm not sure what. She gave up her job at the hospital and that's when she opened the studio."

"Hmm." Before I could ask more about what happened, Bri was walking toward the pool.

"It's kind of cold for that," I said, flinching at how prudish I sounded.

"You sound like my mother. Look, I just want to get my feet wet. The water looks too good to ignore."

I watched Bri as she rolled up her pant legs, plopped down by the side of the pool and plunged both legs into the glass-like water.

Fuck it. I squatted beside her, took off my shoes and dipped my toes in to check the temperature.

"We should get in the hot tub instead," I suggested, glancing over at the curls of steam rising out through the sides of the tub cover.

When I looked over at Bri, her face looked stone cold serious; hard and sober all of a sudden.

"So, you're best friends with my future sister. Tell me something about her that I don't know," Bri said, slyly, curling her lips.

Chapter Ten

TINSLEY

The cousin

As soon as Rosalee closed her bedroom door behind us, she collapsed on the bed, belly first. At first, I thought, in horror, that she might be laughing. But then I realized she was sobbing.

"Oh my god, Rosalee. Georgia will be okay. She's at the hospital and she's stable. Delfina just confirmed it. And I'm sure she's in good hands with your mother-in-law by her side." Truthfully, with what little contact I'd had so far with Asher's mother, Elizabeth had confirmed what I'd suspected from her pics on Facebook. She was cold, a snob, and didn't seem too fond of Rosalee. But now was not the time to criticize my cousin's future mother-in-law.

I sat down on the fluffy, white bed beside Rosalee, remembering all those nights, so long ago, when we'd sat in the bed side by side sharing our nights and our secrets...

Rosalee rolled onto her back, rubbing her face hard, too hard, with her hands. Perhaps she had drunk more champagne than I realized.

"Seriously, she will be okay. I'm sorry this happened. I hope you don't feel like your party is ruined..."

"Tinsley, stop." Rosalee rose up on her elbows, nose dripping with snot. "It's not that. I mean, it is... I hope she's okay and I'm relieved to hear that she's stable. But there's so much more... so much more on my mind."

"Like what?" I leaned in closer and wiped her nose with the hem of my long-sleeved shirt. Rosalee had always been a crier, even when she was young. While I kept my feelings to myself, hers often came flowing out. "Talk to me," I told my cousin.

"It's that." Rosalee pointed over at the gold, woven basket, the one she had been presented with at dinner filled with well wishes from all of us. I'd known about the basket, but like everything else, Mara had taken charge and planned it.

"While everyone else was running outside to wait for the ambulance, I rushed upstairs with those. I didn't want anyone to see..." Rosalee hesitated, still pointing shakily at the letters.

"See what, exactly?" I pressed.

"Look for yourself." Rosalee leaned her head over at the basket.

As I reached inside, she put out her hand to stop me. "Wait. First, I want you to tell me what your message said. I need to know which one you wrote, Tinsley."

I thought about it for a minute, trying to recall the exact words. "Well, I don't know it word for word, but it's the one you read out loud. I wrote something cheesy like, 'Don't go to bed angry. Blah blah blah…'"

"Thank god," Rosalee said, breathily.

"Why? What did you think I wrote?"

Rosalee sighed and slumped back on the pillows. "I wasn't sure. I just needed to know… that it wasn't you who wrote those terrible things."

I grabbed the basket off the nightstand and dumped the square, white notes on the fluffy bedspread. As I unfolded them, one by one, Rosalee tore the heads off the daisies on the comforter beside her, ripping the petals to shreds.

"Okay, here is mine," I said. I pushed the note forward into her hand, the one about going to bed angry. "And this one seems nice… Maybe Mara wrote it?" I couldn't imagine Mara ever being nice, but she did seem fond of my cousin, at least. I pointed a finger at the second note that read:

NEVER STOP GROWING AND WORKING ON YOURSELF AS AN INDIVIDUAL. YOU AND YOUR HUSBAND DESERVE TO HAVE YOUR OWN INTERESTS AND HOBBIES.

Although the words were kind, it seemed exactly like something a self-centered, self-involved person like Mara would come up with off-the-cuff.

The third note made me roll my eyes, but it wasn't all bad:

ALWAYS SMILE IN THE MORNINGS, IT BRIGHTENS YOUR HUSBAND'S DAY AND YOURS TOO!!!!

All those exclamation points made me think it had to be Georgia. But what did I know about her really? Besides the fact that she was seriously allergic to coconut, and she had a body like a pageant queen.

"Okay," I said, looking up at Rosalee, still clutching the note that I suspected came from peppy, polite Georgia.

"It's the last two notes I'm concerned about," Rosalee said.

I unfolded both of them and laid them out, side by side.

KEEP HIM SEXUALLY SATISFIED SO I DON'T HAVE
TO ANYMORE.

"Holy shit," I muttered.

"Believe it or not, the last one is bad too." Rosalee
nodded towards the final 'well wish' in the basket and I
opened it up to read it for myself:

I KNOW ALL OF YOUR SECRETS AND SOON YOUR
HUSBAND WILL TOO.

I gasped. "What the hell? Who are these people you
invited to your party, Rosalee?" I said, waving the note
at her.

"Well, at first I thought that maybe you wrote that
one," Rosalee said, studying my face.

"Me?" My eyes bulged. "How could you think it was
me? Why would I write something like that?"

"I didn't think you would. It's just… you're the only
one who knows my secret. You know how my parents
really died. That was the first thing that came to mind,"
Rosalee said, softly.

I shook my head. "I can't believe you just said that."

"I'm sorry, Tinsley. I don't know what to think. I can't
believe someone, some *people*, would ruin my party this
way. Obviously, two of them are messing with me."

I scooted closer to my cousin, tapping her elbow

gently. "You just said I know your secret, so why would I need to remind you I know in an anonymous note which was going to be shared with these people, or your husband for that matter. I barely know him, or the rest of these women," I said.

Rosalee chewed on her bottom lip, a habit she'd had ever since I met her.

She said, "I know. And I'm sorry for thinking that it was you. I shouldn't have told you that, but you know I'm always honest with you."

"Yeah…" I said.

"But I do think I know who wrote this one." Rosalee pointed at the one that mentioned keeping Asher 'sexually satisfied'.

"Georgia?" I guessed. I didn't know Asher's best friend well, but I'd immediately picked up on the tension between her and my cousin at dinner, especially coming from Rosalee.

Rosalee nodded and pointed at the typed words. "Obviously, Asher's mom and sister aren't messing around with him, and I don't think you or Mara would do that to me. So, that only leaves Georgia. And I've suspected something was going on between her and Asher for a while now…"

"You have?" I said, flabbergasted. I'd noticed the tension between Asher and Georgia, but I hadn't expected a possible affair. "Why would you agree to marry someone if you thought he was being unfaithful, Rosalee? That makes no sense." My cousin was kind, beautiful, and talented. She deserved a man she could fully trust, and one who trusted her back.

Rosalee lowered her eyes. "Because I love him, okay? And because I wanted to trust him when he told me they were only friends. But then I found out that he recently bought a monthly membership to her new gym. And who else could have written that note?"

I scratched at a scab on my arm and tried to think hard about it. "What if…?"

Rosalee raised her eyebrows at me. "Don't even suggest Mara…"

I shook my head. "I don't think highly of Mara, but if anything, she's loyal when it comes to you. No, I was thinking that maybe Elizabeth or Bri wrote it. What better way to stir up trouble than to write something like that? They don't strike me as the friendliest of people, and no offense, but they seem to like Georgia more than you."

"Ugh. I know," Rosalee moaned, falling back on the pillows again. "I just want to go home," she said, miserably.

I lay down beside her, turning my face toward hers.

"You can't run away now, Rosalee. You and I both know that the only way to deal with bullies is to stand up to them. We will find out who wrote these things, the secrets and the sex advice … Do you know what? I'm not even sure if I believe either one of them is serious. They seem petty and mean, like something someone who wanted to stir up drama would say."

"Speaking of stirring up drama, do you think Mara purposefully overlooked the coconut allergy because she doesn't like Georgia?" Rosalee asked, still gnawing at her lip.

I grimaced. "I know Mara's your best friend, but she's a total bitch, Rosalee. I'm sorry to say that…"

Rosalee surprised me with a chuckle. "I know, I know. Mara can be a bitch, but she was a good friend to me in college. I missed you so much when I was gone, and she was all I had then."

"You missed me?" This was the first time I'd heard Rosalee talk about having regrets when it came to leaving me behind.

"I did." Rosalee leaned her head on my chest and closed her eyes. I closed mine too, imagining we were kids again, back in Mom's townhouse, Mom just a few rooms away. We were so safe and secure then, at least for a little while.

Moments later, Rosalee was purring like a kitten. I opened my eyes and stared at the ceiling, unsure what to think of it all.

Chapter Eleven

ROSALEE

The bride-to-be

When I opened my eyes, it took a few minutes to remember where I was and what I was supposed to be doing.

The digital clock on the bedside table read 2:17 a.m. I sat up in the fluffy, white bed and shoved the heavy quilted blankets aside. My temples throbbed and my stomach ached; instantly, it all came rushing back: the champagne and all that food, Georgia's allergic reaction, those horrible anonymous warnings. No, not warnings. They were definitely threats.

I'd fallen asleep with my cousin Tinsley at my side hours ago, but she was nowhere to be seen now. I stood up slowly, blinking in the dark, and tried to use the moonlit shadows to guide me. It took a minute to find the light switch for my room.

I guessed Tinsley had tucked me in and flipped the lights out, just like the old days.

I'd fallen asleep in the clothes I'd been wearing for dinner; they felt sweaty and stiff on my limbs, but I didn't want to change. Instead, I opened my bedroom door and crept down the hall.

The door to Tinsley's room was closed tight, as were Bri and Mara's. I moved quietly, barely breathing, and stood in front of the slightly open doorway that led to Georgia's room. I nudged it with my foot, revealing a perfectly made bed with Georgia's fancy carry-on and matching suitcase still laid out on top. The lamp beside her bed shone brightly.

I couldn't believe she wasn't back from the hospital yet. I hoped that wasn't a bad sign that her reaction was worse than I'd thought. The hospital had reported that she was stable though.

Next to Georgia's room, Elizabeth's door was closed. I knocked lightly and when no one answered, I turned the knob and let myself in. Like Georgia's room, it was empty and well-lit; neither women had returned since leaving in the ambulance hours ago.

Good. I had time then.

Quietly, I moved back to Georgia's room and slipped inside. I hesitated behind the thick wooden doorway, trying to decide if I should lock the door behind me, or not. They weren't here, but I didn't want one of the other ladies coming down the hallway to catch me snooping.

Decisively, I flicked the bolt on the door and moved to Georgia's bedside. I flipped through the contents of her suitcase, the soft T-shirts and deliberately holey jeans, the summery dresses and slacks. Every piece of clothing had her scent on it—patchouli and jasmine.

Next, I sifted through her carry-on. Nothing suspicious there either: makeup and deodorant, a few tampons, a toothbrush, floss and birth control pills.

She was as boring and simple as she was pretty, I guess.

I'd been hoping for her cell phone, but it was possible she took it with her.

I hadn't seen her with a purse, but her wallet had to be somewhere…

Opening the bedside drawers, I found nothing. But when I opened the closet, thick with dust, and pulled the light string to illuminate the space, I saw her wallet, a set of keys, and a black shiny cell phone resting on the top shelf.

I reached for the cell phone, breathlessly. If she was having an affair with my fiancé, the proof should be right here.

But as soon as I flipped the phone over, I caught a flash of a partial unread message on her screen. I gasped.

YOU DESERVE TO DIE FOR WHAT YOU DID, BITCH.

I tried to click on the message to read the rest but was instantly prompted to scan my fingerprint.

"Shit," I hissed, swiping back and forth and up and down, trying to see the messages again.

This time, the phone prompted me for a six-digit password. There were too many potential combinations, and I didn't know anything about Georgia, not really. I didn't even know her birthday, which was sad considering she was supposedly my fiancé's best friend.

I put the phone back on the shelf, a shiver running through me. I hadn't recognized the number on the message, and now that I'd unsuccessfully tried to unlock the home screen, I could no longer see it displayed. But that message… that certainly wasn't from a friend, or some sort of prank.

Similarly, with my 'well wishes', there was someone threatening Georgia. I wondered what she'd done to make someone that angry.

Chapter Twelve

ELIZABETH

The mother-in-law

My hands were shaking as I lifted the heavy pot of coffee and poured myself a full cup. I lifted the brew to my lips and sipped, enjoying the burning sensation on my tongue and the roof of my mouth. A punishment that was well-deserved felt good sometimes.

I'd barely slept a wink since returning to the mansion at half past three that morning. Georgia, after all the antihistamines and cortisol, was exhausted, barely able to trudge up the stairs and fall into bed.

But me, I couldn't shake off the feelings of fear and regret in my chest.

It's impossible to break a heart, in reality. But certain things, certain events, can certainly break a person.

Losing my beloved husband fractured something in me. And sitting in that hospital waiting room last night, hour after hour, waiting for Georgia... all I could do was sit and think about the last time I'd been in a room like that.

Edmund had suffered from heart issues since his mid-forties. A stint here, a valve replacement there, ablation surgeries and tweaking his pacemaker as he grew older. Waiting around during his surgeries and procedures had become like second nature to me. In fact, I'd been downright annoyed by him that evening before. I'd wanted to go out to a local event at our church and he hadn't felt up to it. *Maybe I should just take myself. You're no fun anymore,* I'd snapped at him.

Maybe you should, Elizabeth, Edmund had said, his voice mopey and sad. We used to go out and do fun things. We used to be fun, happy people...

I'd rolled my eyes and spent the evening watching news programs on TV while he rested.

That next morning, he didn't feel any better. Again, I thought he was overreacting—over the years, he'd become overly health conscious, which was good for his heart but sometimes aggravating to deal with as his partner. I liked eating red meat and drinking alcohol, thank you very much.

I drove him to the ER, quieter than usual. I was still stewing over the missed church party, as though it were anything important, really. Looking back, it was a stupid event filled with stupid people. And I should have spent the evening with my darling husband, comforting him.

But I didn't know. I didn't.

And when the ER doctor told me that he had a blockage, I wasn't all that shocked about that either. Edmund had gone through this so many times, and his doctors were great at what they did. I'd come to assume that his stubborn heart could survive anything...

When the doctors found me, I was sitting in the waiting room doing a crossword puzzle, my phone tucked between my cheek and shoulder, chatting with one of my girlfriends from church.

I talked for a few more minutes, making the young, sheepish-looking doctor wait for me to finish my conversation.

And when I hung up and tucked my crossword away, I asked him how many more hours I'd have to wait until I could take Edmund home. That's when he told me— Edmund was gone.

I would never get to take my husband home again.

All that time, chatting and complaining, configuring my stupid letters into words, my husband lay in there dying. I didn't even tell him goodbye before he went back to surgery. I didn't kiss his lips or squeeze his hand. I didn't tell my husband I loved him one last time.

So, sitting there in that room last night, waiting on Georgia, I felt myself reliving that day, over and over again, the rush of shock and regret. His words coming back to me as I moaned about going out to parties alone… *Maybe you should, Elizabeth.*

It had been three years. I knew that I should be over it. Hell, I'd even had younger friends point out that 'at least he had a good, long life', as though getting older made it any less hard to lose the love of your life. I hated them for trying to comfort me, for trying to blubber over their pleasantries and 'sorry for your loss's, for their explanations as to why my husband had to leave my side. He left for no good reason, and I failed to say goodbye or give him any comfort there at the end. I deserved to be sad and lonely.

I finished my coffee, throat scorched, and poured myself another cup. The catering staff had been kind enough to leave some breakfast foods, but I wasn't much of an eater these days. Nothing tasted good and meals without Edmund were depressing.

"There you are. I was so worried…" Rosalee slipped inside the kitchen, sneaky like a snake. Her eyes were puffy, and her hair was uncombed. *What does my son see in this girl?* I wondered for the millionth time.

"We got in late. After three in the morning," I grumbled.

"I'm surprised you didn't sleep in then. How's Georgia?" Rosalee asked.

She picked up a baguette and took a large bite of it. She didn't look too worried, if you ask me.

"Fine. They gave her a cocktail of things to calm her down, put her on oxygen. She was lucky, you know. Your friend really screwed up there."

Rosalee stopped chewing and stared.

"I'm sorry. I think it was just an honest mistake," she said, struggling to swallow the thick, seed-filled bread. *The last thing she needs is carbs,* I thought, eyes trailing down to her bulging waistline and thighs.

"Well, I hope it won't happen again. I'd hate for Asher to lose his closest friend over something so easily avoided," I said.

Rosalee lowered her eyes but said nothing.

The doors to the kitchen swung open again; Bri and Mara came in, chatting amiably until they saw Rosalee and me.

"Oh. Hi there. How's Georgia?" Mara asked, energetically. *Fine. No thanks to you,* I wanted to say.

"Fine. Just sleeping it off." Speaking of sleeping it off, I made eyes at my daughter. She had acted like a drunken fool last night, polishing off two bottles of wine on her own before the dessert menu had even arrived.

I'd like to think that I was surprised, but really, I wasn't. I stopped by her apartment a few times a month to pick up parcels. She was so busy with work most days, and I liked to be helpful. Additionally, it gave me a chance to snoop...

I saw the bottles she tried to hide. The full bottles in her cupboards and cabinets. The empty bottles buried in her waste basket and out in the garbage can at the curb. And the prescriptions for anxiety pills that seemed to run out faster than the doctor intended...

As I shook off concerns about my daughter's drug and alcohol use, I realized that Mara was still looking at me and talking. "Well, the plan for today was for us to get a cab and head into town. I thought we could explore Jackson Square and the open markets down there. Then at two, I have a masseuse and makeup lady coming, to get us all relaxed and get Rosalee dolled up for a night out on the town. The cooking staff are returning to prepare appetizers for later..." Mara blabbed on and on about her agenda.

"That all sounds great, but I'm not leaving Georgia here." I lifted my coffee cup and blew steam off the top.

"Well, why don't I stay here with her?" Mara offered. "You, Bri, Tinsley, and Rosalee can go have some fun, and I'll wait on Georgia hand and foot. It's the least I can do."

I was tempted to tell her the truth—that I wouldn't trust her to take care of my pet dog (if I owned one, which I absolutely do not; dogs are slobbery, loathsome creatures).

"No. That's quite all right. I'm tired and I would prefer to stay in while you young ones go out and have fun," I said, truthfully.

Mara shrugged. "Okay, if you insist."

"I do," I said, giving her a stern glance. I still wasn't sure if the coconut incident was an accident or done out of spite. Like Rosalee, surely Mara could see that Georgia posed a threat to her friend and Asher's marriage. Georgia was much better suited for my son and I'd be damned if I let that loudmouth Mara try to harm her again.

I watched the others filter out of the kitchen and drift back upstairs to get ready for their fun day out. *Good riddance*, I thought, tossing my cup in the sink.

Chapter Thirteen

BRI

The sister-in-law

As much as I loved my mother, a day spent exploring New Orleans without her by my side sounded pretty good.

It wasn't hard to miss the St. Louis Cathedral, nestled in the heart of Jackson Square, overlooking the neighboring historic buildings and neighborhoods. With its towers, spires, majestic clock, and church bells, it inspired awe, even from a non-history buff like me.

Of course, Tinsley had a lot to tell us, in her mousy, shy voice—the history behind the cathedral's original construction in the sixteenth century, and about the fire and calamities it suffered through the years. *Blah, blah, blah.* That girl was boring!

As much as the old cathedral intrigued me, it was what was around it that really drew me in. Crowds of people were gathered in the square, some shopping at small pop-up booths, others dancing or playing music.

"Look! There's a wedding parade," Rosalee gushed. I turned to where she and the others were pointing. A brass band came marching right through the square, cornets and trombones blaring, leading a line of partygoers behind them. They were all dancing and smiling happily, and through the line-up I could see the tiny bride in a long, white dress and her handsome, grinning groom beside her.

"Wow. Should have gotten married here, instead of that stuffy Merribelle Gardens," Mara said, clapping along and waving at the line of people.

I rolled my eyes. As much fun as I'd had hanging out with Mara at the pool last night, she was quick to remind me that she could be as annoying as hell.

"Nothing compares to Merribelle Gardens and don't let my mother hear you saying things like that, Rosalee," I said, turning my back on the parade and walking toward a stream of tents filled with booths.

The French Market reminded me a bit of Europe, with the open-air stalls and the handmade souvenirs. *It's like an overpriced flea market without any air conditioning*, I thought, haughtily.

There was something awful in the air, a mixture of old burlap, meat, and funeral flowers.

"Wait up." Mara again. Great.

"Tinsley and Rosalee spotted a palm reader," Mara said, ducking under the tent to join me. There were stalls and tables packed in tightly; people selling a collection of shit. Graphic T-shirts, handmade soaps, and candles. Bottles full of sand, beaded jewelry, and bags of homemade sweets.

"I don't want to get my palm read," I said, stopping at one of the stalls with Christmas ornaments made out of blown glass. The woman behind the table flashed a big smile, showing off a mouthful of metal piercings. *Just what I always wanted. Ornaments in April,* I thought, shrilly. Mom would have hated this place. Good thing she hung back at the mansion with Georgia.

"Me neither," Mara, said, falling in step beside me. We strolled through the market, which was remarkably crowded, even for a Saturday morning, during non-carnival season. I hadn't expected to see so many people.

As I glanced at their faces, I realized I couldn't tell them apart—locals from tourists.

This seemed like the sort of place you could blend right in and disappear, but also find community if you really wanted to.

Perhaps when Mom was gone, I could move to a place

more like this one. Streets filled with noise and color, unlike our secluded farm roads back home where everybody knew each other. A place filled with people and things to do. A place where Mom wasn't around judging my every move.

I stopped at a table with a cooler of soft drinks and paid four bucks for a bottle of Coke. I was still suffering from a mild hangover, less from the alcohol itself—I was used to that—and more from mixing it with too many pills. I held the cool soft drink to my cheeks and forehead, rolling it around.

"Want a soda?" I said, turning to look over at Mara who was bent over a table inspecting a dainty piece of beaded jewelry, while chatting amiably with the young man working behind the stall.

She glanced over, pointed at my drink, and rolled her eyes.

"Thank you," she told the boy and walked back over to me.

"What do you say we get out of here and get a real drink?" she suggested.

"Isn't it kind of early?" I said, looking around at all the strangers. It *was* early, but it wasn't too early for me. Not too early to get a little buzz going…

"Hell no, it's not too early!" Mara said. "You know what they say about the hair of the dog, and the best cure for a hangover, don't you?" She wiggled her eyebrows and smiled. As much as I didn't want to, I was starting to like this girl.

"What about Rosalee and Tinsley?" I asked.

Mara frowned and glanced out across the causeway, as though she could see the women from here. "I'm not too worried about them. Let's give the cousins time to catch up today. We'll meet back up with them at the house later. Sound good?"

"Sounds perfect," I smiled.

Chapter Fourteen

GEORGIA

The groom's friend

When I opened my eyes, I was in a bright white room. I blinked the sun away, yawned, and sat up in the four-poster bed.

I was still wearing my jeans and T-shirt from last night. The material stuck to my chest and waist; my whole body was drenched in sweat. I turned my hand over and frowned at the band on my wrist. The hospital. The coconut. My damn allergic reaction…

Groaning, I climbed out of bed and stripped off my clothes. My head felt heavy and foggy, all the antihistamines still lingering in my system. I knew for sure that I'd told Mara I was allergic to coconut. Had she forgotten to tell the cooking staff, or did someone give me the coconut on purpose?

It was obvious that Mara and Rosalee didn't trust me, considering my relationship with Asher. But trying to send me into anaphylactic shock on purpose? That seemed a little extreme...

For a brief moment I considered something worse— what if this was somehow related to the messages I'd been receiving? Could they be behind this somehow?

My skin felt itchy and hot, my blood pressure rising as my daily anxious existence came floating back to me as it did most mornings.

I went to the window and threw open the balcony doors to let a beam of sunlight stream in. Despite the immediate warmth, I could see dark clouds gathering over the pool and courtyard. The smell of storms in the air...

Most mornings, I started my day with a simple ten-minute yoga sequence to de-stress and I shared it with my online followers so they could follow along at home if they wanted to.

But lately, I'd found it harder and harder to concentrate, and even stretching out my daily routines wasn't having the calming effects they used to.

I'd discovered yoga and fitness while in college and it had become such a necessary part of my daily life, almost like a drug—my body needed the tension and relief it provided. I'd also grown accustomed to the praise, support, and community I received from my followers online, which was one of the main reasons I decided to open the gym.

But lately, the comment section, much like my phone, had become an uncomfortable place.

One glance in the mirror revealed that my face was still red and swollen from the reaction last night. I considered filming anyway and revealing details about my reaction to coconut.

But what if it was one of them? No one was safe anymore.

I opted not to make a video this time and I went through the motions of my workout, barely feeling it. As suspected, I didn't feel much better when I was done.

I closed the curtains and slipped on a loose dress. In the rush of my emergency last night, I'd left my cell phone and other belongings behind in the closet. I opened the closet door and reached for my phone.

It was sitting on the shelf, face up, the screen flickering and buzzing as notifications came in.

Someone had messed with my phone, I realized in horror, hand stopped mid-air as I reached for it.

I was a creature of habit and for the past year, I'd developed a habit of always leaving my phone face down, somewhere I couldn't see it. It helped me avoid distractions while working at the gym, but also it helped me avoid seeing the awful, threatening messages I'd been receiving via texts and online.

There was no way I would have left it face up. No way...

But when I picked it up, the screen was still locked. No one knew my code and there was absolutely no way someone got in and snooped through my phone. I chastised myself. I was just being paranoid...

Perhaps it was just the cleaning staff that moved it. Or perhaps I'd gotten lazy in my normal routine due to all the stress and anxiety.

Flipping through nearly a dozen messages, I was fraught to discover they were all from the same person. More threats. More taunting. If they'd had it their way, I'd have been left for dead after eating all that stupid cake last night.

I put the phone back on the shelf where it belonged —*face down*. As I emerged from my room, I found the hallway deserted. Moving from room to room, I peeked in at all the empty beds.

Rosalee and Elizabeth had made their beds, corners tucked in neatly. But the other women had not.

Poor Elizabeth. She was a nervous wreck when we came back to the mansion last night. I wondered if she at least got some sleep after sitting at the hospital half the night.

Down the twisty staircase, I made my way to the first

level of the house. I was met with more silence, like I was walking through a tomb or the inside of a vacuum.

I had the strangest thought—that perhaps I'd died, after all, and now I was just a lonely ghost, wandering these halls for eternity.

But then a woman with the biggest hair I'd ever seen came bursting around the corner and I leapt back in surprise.

"Oh!" She held a hand to her chest. "You scared the shit out of me, doll! I wasn't expecting anyone to be here."

"Are you … part of the help?" I asked. Was she the one who messed with my phone? Flutters of paranoia returned.

The woman looked at me with a confused expression and laughed. "I mean, I guess you could say that. I don't work here, though. Mara Mattingly paid me to be here. I'm doing massages for the bridal party and my co-workers are coming to do the bride-to-be's hair and makeup in a bit. I was setting up my tables… and then I ran into you! Are you by chance Miss Mara?"

I shook my head. "No, I'm sorry. I'm Georgia. I wasn't feeling well, so I slept in late … I guess the others are gone?"

"I guess so. I'm Angie. Nice to meet you, Georgia. Such a peachy name, like that song!"

I swallowed, my throat still dry from all the heaving and gasping. "Yep. Like that song…"

"Well, if it's okay with you, I'm going to go set up now. I won't be in your way, will I? The massages are at two," she said, in a pleasant, chirpy voice.

I shook my head. "No, that's fine. And I'll try to stay out of your way too."

I wandered to the dining room. The long wooden table had been scrubbed and polished, nothing left behind to remind me of last night's party. The kitchen, so full of staff last night, was now sterile and deserted.

I found a jug of milk in the fridge, poured myself a bowl of cheerios, and carried it through the kitchen and down the long dark hallway, letting myself out onto the private, semi-hidden courtyard behind the house.

Moments after settling in at one of the small wrought-iron tables, I heard a brush of movement through the archway, then the unmistakable splash of water. I stood and moved to the gate, surprised to see Elizabeth Beake swimming laps in the pool.

Her white hair was pulled back in a tight chignon and she wore a shimmery black one-piece bathing suit that somehow showed off her aging, yet trim and athletic figure.

She was moving gracefully from one side of the pool to the other, taking long and quick strokes. Her neck was smooth, swan-like. She had always been an elegant woman.

"I wish I had your energy," I said, leaving my forgotten breakfast and taking a seat at one of the lounge chairs beside the pool.

Elizabeth swam over to the side, inches from my manicured toes, and propped herself up on her elbows at the edge. "Feeling better, then? Get some rest?"

"Yeah. All better," I sighed. Physically, I was fine. Emotionally, I was stressed as fuck. But it's not like I could say that to Asher's prim and proper mother.

"Are you okay?" I asked her. Last night, she had been in a whole other world, ghost-white and silent, fearful. Not like the confident, bordering on arrogant, Elizabeth I'd known most of my life.

"Of course. I was just worried about you, that's all," Elizabeth waved me off.

But she was lying, of course. I could tell last night that she was struggling; the stark hospital walls and that hellish waiting room she must have been stuck in for hours. It probably reminded her of Edmund.

They had been lovely together in many ways. My childhood was sprinkled with memories of Asher's parents—dancing in the kitchen, half-drunk on bourbon, at their yearly Christmas party. Edmund was always giving her gifts. And the way that man looked at her, like she was the only woman in the world, his eyes lusty and loving even after all those years.

Their relationship was certainly different than that of my parents, and I usually enjoyed being at Asher's house more than my own.

"No need to worry. I'm fine now," I told her.

"How about Asher? Have you talked to him? Did you tell him what happened?" Elizabeth pushed.

I tugged on my hair, using the hair tie on my wrist to slip it into a flimsy bun. There had been a chilly breeze coming home in the early hours of the morning, but now the sun peeking through the clouds felt startling, burning down on my shoulders and neck.

"I texted him yesterday, but no, I didn't tell him about the allergy incident. The last thing I want is to worry him. This event is supposed to be a celebration for Rosalee, and I don't want to do anything to ruin it for her, or for Asher," I said.

Elizabeth turned, circling her arms widely in the water. She looked both bird-like and beautiful, all at once. I knew we were supposed to be afraid of aging, but there was something lovely about it. I just hoped I aged like Elizabeth, and not like my own mother, my memories of her fading more and more every day…

"Well, if she didn't want her party ruined, then she shouldn't have put that self-centered Mara in charge.

Can you believe she overlooked your allergy? I worry it was done intentionally."

"I doubt that," I lied. I was definitely still considering it—did Rosalie's best friend consider me a threat, and try to hurt me or humiliate me by offering cake she knew would make me sick? Or was there someone else behind it?

I forced myself to consider the third, and most reasonable, option—that it was all an accident, a misunderstanding, just like Mara claimed.

"I don't doubt it was purposeful, not even for a second! And you shouldn't either, Georgia," Elizabeth said, standing upright in the pool. She gave me a serious look.

"But what reason would Mara have for trying to hurt me?" I said wearily, rubbing my eyes with the palm of my hands. I'd been around Elizabeth so many times throughout my life, at family dinners and while visiting Asher, and she visited my mom every so often to check on her. But rarely did I ever find myself completely alone with the woman. For some reason, it was making me slightly uncomfortable, and I fought the urge to get up and walk away from her.

"Come on, Georgia. You and I both know that people have always suspected you and Asher were more than friends…"

"It's not like that," I protested.

But now Elizabeth was pulling herself out of the pool, saddling herself up next to my chair. She looked surprisingly strong, her arms flexing as they glistened in the bright white sun.

"I love you like a daughter, you know that," Elizabeth said.

I wished like crazy that I had something to cover up my face—a big pair of sunglasses or a bandanna. Anything to hide the discomfort that had to be written all over it right now.

"I know you do, Elizabeth," I said.

"Your mother was my best friend. She still is." Elizabeth's eyes were wet, but I couldn't tell if it was water dripping down from her hair or actual tears.

Mother never cries, Asher told me once. *If you opened up her chest, I bet you'd find all wires and gadgets in there. She's hardwired to be tough, always has been.*

"I know," I said again, reaching out to touch her arm. I wished more than anything that I could go back to those days, my mom and Elizabeth, thick as thieves, drinking and playing cards at the kitchen table. But Mom had been diagnosed with Alzheimer's three years ago, right around the time of Edmund's death; the disease had quickly wiped away the woman I remembered as my mother, and that Elizabeth remembered as her dearest friend.

"I want Asher to be happy," Elizabeth said, giving me a knowing look.

"I want that too," I said. "And he adores Rosalee, you must know that."

Elizabeth looked off into the distance, shading her eyes with a hand as she stared into the sun.

"I think he cares for her, yes. But if there's something between the two of you, I need to know it. Before I give my blessing to all of this ... I have to know if you're in love with my son. Please, Georgia. I need to know the truth, if not from him then from you."

A roll of clouds was moving through the sky, fighting to blot out the sun completely. A storm was coming, I could feel it. Even as a little girl, I could always sense the rain before it hit. My mother thought I could smell it, something brewing in the air...

Elizabeth wanted to know the truth, but how much should I tell her?

I took a deep breath and opened my mouth. Then I told her the truth about my feelings for Asher.

Chapter Fifteen

ROSALEE

The bride-to-be

By the time my cousin and I made it back to the Leblanc-Landry mansion, we were drenched from head to toe, our shopping and food bags soggy from the sudden downpour.

"Christ, it's freezing in here!" Tinsley shivered, closing the door behind us. The rain was whipping up a frenzy outside, rattling the windows and doors.

I slid out of my tennis shoes and set my bags down in the foyer, teeth chattering. "Damn, it is cold in here."

The chill felt so unexpected in the New Orleans heat but getting caught in the sudden rain on our walk back from the square had left us water-logged and helpless.

"I knew we should have called a cab." Tinsley shuffled her bags next to mine and smiled.

"It was fun though. I love this city. I could walk around this place all day every day, minus the downpour," I said.

"Me too," Tinsley agreed.

"I hope Bri and Mara were smart enough to find a cab though."

"Knowing them, they're probably still down at the bar getting sloshed." Tinsley frowned. Any time I had mentioned Mara on our outing today, I'd been met with clear distaste from Tinsley.

I nodded toward the hallway and collected our bags. "Let's go get into something dry."

We made our way down the dark hallway. Candles flickered in their holders, shadows dancing along the corners of the walls. I couldn't imagine being able to go out on the town tonight, not in this sort of weather. But I knew so little about New Orleans' weather patterns—I hoped it was like Florida, and the storm would pass as suddenly as it had arrived.

"Oh." Tinsley stopped so suddenly in the great room as we approached the stairs, that I stepped on the back of her heels.

I followed her gaze. One of the large sunrooms was open, and two women, half-clothed, were lying on their stomachs, having massages.

"There you are," Elizabeth said, turning her face over to give me a sideways scowl. A voluptuous woman with a huge head of hair was towering over Asher's mother, knuckling her bare shoulders and back.

"Here we are," Tinsley said, a flash of annoyance on her face. "I thought the massages weren't for another hour or two."

"Sorry, miss. We got here early, so we decided to get started. I've already massaged your other two friends, Bri and Mara? And after we're done with these two, it will be y'all's's turn," the masseuse said, with a practiced smile.

I was surprised to hear that Bri and Mara had beat us back to the house. Almost as surprised as I was to see them hanging out together. I adored Mara, but something about her buddying up with Bri, after I told her how cold Asher's sister had been to me, didn't feel right. Especially in light of those obnoxious letters I received last night. I couldn't help but wonder what she was up to. Why was she suddenly so interested in Bri?

"No thanks. I'll pass on the massage," Tinsley said, shifting her bags to her other hip. To me, she said, "I'm going upstairs to shower and change."

As she headed for the stairs, I stepped further into the room. Georgia was lying on the other table beside Elizabeth, hair fanned around her head like a bright sunny halo. I couldn't see her glowing face. My thoughts drifted back to that ugly message on her cell phone last night. Who was threatening her and why?

"Are you feeling better, Georgia?" I said, tentatively. But she didn't answer.

"I think she fell asleep," her small, dark-headed masseuse said, giving me an apologetic smile. She was rubbing Georgia's shoulders softly, as though she were a big, cuddly baby lying on the table. I couldn't help noticing how fit her shoulders and calve muscles were, bringing back thoughts of Asher, hanging out at her yoga studio with his gym membership.

"Georgia's fine. Just tired," Elizabeth said. She turned her head in the other direction, dismissing me.

"Bri and Mara already returned?" I asked.

"Yes. They're upstairs with the makeup artist, picking out nail colors, I believe. They were quite … rowdy," the blonde masseuse said. She was busy kneading, leaning her whole body into Elizabeth's bony backside.

I headed upstairs to get changed, eager to strip out of my clothes and towel off, I was annoyed to find both Bri and Mara in my room, alongside another woman I didn't know.

"Oh, hi there! I'm LeeAnn!" The woman practically accosted me, pumping my hand up and down before I could barely put my bags away. "Congrats on your wedding!" she boomed. "I'm LeeAnn," she repeated, "and I'm here to do your hair and makeup for a fun night out with the girls. Your friends here were just debating what colors go best with your outfit."

"My outfit?" I said, wearily.

Mara rushed over to the bed, holding up a soft, petal-pink sundress with matching shoes. "We picked this out for you. See? I thought maybe gold polish and gold makeup highlights, because it has some gold accents on it." She pointed at the tiny gold buttons leading down the dress and the gold straps on the shoes. It was a lovely dress, I had to admit.

"This… Did you buy this for me?" I spoke.

"Sure did. Well, Bri paid for it. But I found it," Mara said happily, pointing over at Bri. Bri gave me a tight, awkward smile.

"Do you like it? I know you don't wear many dresses, but I wanted to get something for you. And I want you to feel like a princess tonight!" Mara said. I noticed her lips were stained blue in the corners and her breath smelled heavily of Malibu rum and tropical flavors. It brought back thoughts of coconut and I cringed. Had Mara really done that on purpose? Her face when I looked across the table and saw her… She had almost looked proud of herself when Georgia collapsed.

"Thank you. I love it," I said, uneasily. I ran my fingers over the soft fabric and fingered the heavy gold straps on the shoes. "I hope we can go out tonight. It's raining so hard. Tinsley and I decided to walk back and got soaked."

"Well, it's supposed to clear up in a few hours," Bri said, lifting a bottle of pink nail polish and turning it over to read the label on the back. "Mind if I borrow this one for myself?" she asked LeeAnn.

"No, of course not! Help yourself, dear!" LeeAnn chimed.

Moments later, they had all cleared out of my room and given me a few minutes to change. I towel-dried my hair and changed into an easy-to-remove, button-down shirt, as LeeAnn had instructed, so as not to mess up my hair when I went to change my clothes later.

LeeAnn was waiting for me in the hallway, her massive makeup case saddled in her hand.

"Are you ready for your Cinderella moment? Did you already do your massage? I don't want to do your hair and makeup if you still need your massage," LeeAnn rambled.

I thought about Georgia and Elizabeth downstairs, having their bonding moment or whatever it was, and felt a flicker of rage in my gut. *Which one of them wrote those notes last night?* I wondered, again.

The trip into town with Tinsley had cheered me up and provided a nice little reprieve from my worries. But now that I was back, I was fixated again—who was trying to sabotage my marriage? And why?

"No. I decided to skip the massage and get right to the beauty part," I said, sitting on the edge of the bed.

LeeAnn started with makeup. "This is called 'beating your face'," she informed me.

"Hmm." I closed my eyes, as instructed, letting her beat my face into submission, toning and shading and doing god knows what.

"Is it okay if I pluck your brows before I do them?" LeeAnn asked, hot minty breath in my face.

"Sure." My brows were thick and awful. I'd never been one of those girls, although I often wished I were, especially when I was younger. What I lacked in style and looks, I tried to make up for with personality.

Thinking back to those awkward teenage years, my breasts too big for my body, my body all weird angles and curves, I couldn't help also thinking of Tinsley. She was naturally gorgeous, taking after her father, I guessed. She looked nothing like her own mother or my father. She tried so hard back then, in high school, trying the lipsticks and the liners, straightening her long white hair like a pin until it singed on the ends. But no matter how pretty she was, her shyness always got the best of her. She tended to blend in, sometimes nearly invisible, and she didn't make friends very easily.

I should have stayed in contact better with her after college. I knew nothing about her life now. I tried to imagine her, still living back there in that townhouse in her hometown of Monroe where we spent the late years of our youth, although all alone now, without her mom or me. *Does she have anyone?* I wondered. I knew she was working at the bookshop still, but what about relationships? Friendships? Had I been so focused on my own drama that I'd failed to think about my cousin's life and how well she was doing without me? I'd spent most of our time together today, talking about myself, I realized, guiltily.

The hours in Jackson Square with her had been the best I'd spent so far since starting the trip. The palm reader told us our future—lots of dark and handsome men, turning points in which we had to make huge, life-changing choices. After we'd tipped the reader handsomely, we'd nearly burst with laughter before we turned the corner.

"Everything those people say could be applied to anyone. It's so... generic," Tinsley said, shaking her head.

"Yeah, I had this amazing psych professor during my sophomore year of college who told us that they're called 'Barnum statements'. I'd never heard that before, the Barnum effect, but apparently, it's when a statement is so vague that you can basically use it to describe anyone. Which is why horoscopes usually make sense when you read them..."

Tinsley had stopped walking; she was digging around in her purse, looking for nothing, a dull expression on her face. "Yeah, that's basically what I just said."

And just like that, I remembered—how much it bothered her that I went to college. How important it was for her to feel smart and heard, and how often I'd talked over her when we were younger.

"I'm sorry. I like to repeat things sometimes," I cringed.

"I know. And that's why I love you," Tinsley nudged my elbow, her face softening. "I've missed having you around, Rosalee. Things haven't been the same without you."

And just like that, the tension between us had dissipated, like it always did when we were together and had minor disagreements in the past. Just like it does with siblings.

"Hold perfectly still," LeeAnn warned me, as she applied sticky, adhesive lashing over the top of my own eyelashes. When she was done, she told me to blink, and she stared right in my face, at exactly my eye level, making sure the lashes were even.

"I'll let you see soon, but not until I've done this hair."

"Okay," I said, giving an awkward laugh. My face felt weird and tight, unused to wearing so much makeup. The plucking hadn't been too painful, but the tender skin around my brows stung a bit.

As LeeAnn set to work on my hair, pulling and twisting with a hot curling iron, I took out my phone and opened my messenger app for the first time since arriving at the Leblanc-Landry mansion. All the messages were from Asher.

He had messaged me early this morning, but I hadn't read it.

How was the flight? How's the weather there? Miss you, Boo. I didn't want to message you yesterday and interrupt your girl time.

Asher had sent a couple more casual messages, then wrote:

I guess you're busy having fun! I'm so glad. You deserve it. Love you. Xoxo

Yesterday, I'd been so bothered by his failure to message me, never considering the fact that he was giving me space to celebrate with my friends. Perhaps I should have messaged him myself when I got in, I thought, guiltily.

I stared at the hugs and kisses in his message, imagining Asher typing them. He was so well-spoken in person, talking to clients and judges and fellow attorneys. But when it came to texting, he often left a lot to be desired. I could picture him sitting alone in our new farmhouse, trying to think about what he should write to please me. Because he knew how much I hated his often abrupt, too short replies.

This afternoon while I was busy with Tinsley, he had sent several more messages.

Look what I'm doing! Got up early and had an idea. We should grow our own garden. Tomatoes and lettuce. Maybe some potatoes? Hell, we could can our own tomatoes, jar our own beans... We could come up with our own family recipe for things like ketchup. Spaghetti sauce! The Mumford-Beake brand! What do you think?

I couldn't help smiling as I scrolled through a couple of pictures he had sent from what was obviously an orange cart from Home Depot. Despite the chilly weather, he was walking around the home store, filling the cart with tiny packets of seeds and bags of soil.

I loved when Asher was like this, excited like a small child, his ability to jump from one task to the next overwhelming but fun.

I liked the idea of a garden. And I especially liked how he had hyphenated my name.

As much as I wanted to be a Beake, I didn't want to give up Mumford either. It was my mother's last name, and being the only Mumford left to carry it on, letting the surname go felt like letting a piece of myself die. I wasn't ready to do that yet…

Before I could respond to the messages about the garden, I scrolled down to the last few he'd sent.

Oops. It's too cold to start the garden and I'll need to rent or buy a tiller first. Plus, I want to wait until you're here to get that started. I was bored without you, so I started doing some unpacking. And I got to looking at your art. Guess what? I found some of your older pieces, in a long white tub that I think came from your last apartment. It looks like it's been packed away for a while. I've never seen some of these before. They're brilliant baby!

The last photo he'd sent was of a stark canvas, red river swirls running through it.

We need to hang this by our Christmas tree in the winter. Reminds me of candy canes and cherry pie.

That had been the last message he'd sent, several hours ago.

I clutched the phone in my hand, oblivious to LeeAnn's fingers, twisting slices of my hair into small braids. It certainly wasn't a painting inspired by

Christmas. It was blood on snow. Head swiveling in the cold. Dark dead eyes staring into mine as skinny little rivers of blood created a trail in the powdery white earth...

"You, okay?" LeeAnn asked, breathy in my ear.

I jerked, feeling the tug of my scalp as my hair snapped back in her thick, working hands.

"Fine. Are we almost done? I'm getting antsy."

It was rude of me, but all I could think of in that moment was Asher. He knew so little about my past. How could I marry him without telling him the truth about what happened to my parents?

Chapter Sixteen

TINSLEY

The cousin

The rain outside was slowing to a drizzle, the soft pings on the glass a soothing soundtrack for the latest book I was reading. Curled up on my bed, I flicked through the sodden pages of one of my favorite weather-worn mystery paperbacks, seeing the words but not really comprehending them.

How could I focus on a fictional mystery when a real-life one was unfolding before me?

I closed the book and went to the window, looking out at the furious sky and the drenched courtyard below.

Bri and Mara were sitting out there, tucked under an umbrella. They had their feet up on the tables (how rude!), and they appeared to be giving themselves pedicures. Their mouths were moving, chatting about something. A couple of empty bottles of wine at their feet.

I rolled my eyes and moved away from the window. Next, I strolled through the hallway, passing by Rosalee's room. Her door was cracked and from there, I could see her poised in a fancy seat at the dressing table. LeeAnn hovered behind her with a bobby pin clenched in her teeth, tightly winding Rosalee's hair.

Silently, I moved through the long dark hallway and down the stairs, passing by the sunroom with the masseuses, Elizabeth, and Georgia. Both women appeared to be sleeping now, Elizabeth snoring like a baby pig.

For a moment, I considered joining them—I'd never had a massage before; they were a luxury I couldn't normally afford—but decided against it. I could have gone into the wet, hazy courtyard and tried to blend in with Mara and Bri, but I had no interest in spending time with them, either. They seemed like they belong together. *Maybe Mara will have a new best friend to replace Rosalee with after this trip*, I thought.

As usual, no one seemed to notice me, as I moved through the house, looking again at the jaw-dropping library and examining the thick, heavy oil paintings on the walls. The Leblanc-Landry mansion was an interesting place. There were no shortages of places with creepy histories in New Orleans, but the Leblanc-Landry one was decidedly darker than usual.

The Landry's were a wealthy, prominent family who bequeathed the estate to their one and only son, William Landry. When he fell in love with a local merchant's daughter, his family was beyond disappointed. But he didn't care, marrying Vivian Landry anyway. Together, they had six beautiful children, and according to local legend, they were the happiest and wealthiest family in town.

But like most families, all the beauty and wealth on the outside couldn't hide the rotting worms from within. Landry's father had pushed her to marry the wealthy man, and although she loved her home and her children, her true love was for another man in town, a local cobbler. When William was working, she snuck her lover inside. For years, they continued their affair. But like all secrets, it was bound to come to light, and one day when William returned early from work and found them together, it did.

William was so distraught that he murdered both his wife and her lover, but he didn't stop there. He also killed all six of his children, one by one, convinced they belonged to the cobbler and not him.

It was a terrible, tragic story but most houses around here had history. If not a personal tragedy, then there was still blood to be found—the South's long history of slavery, and before that, the lands stained red with the blood of Native Americans. It's impossible to go anywhere without some sort of dark, devious history attached to it.

Downstairs, I moved from room to room, tapping on walls like I was a kid again—Nancy Drew-esque, always searching for something hidden in the walls, but rarely finding it. The dining room was deserted, but through the windows, I could see Bri and Mara still by the pool, talking and drinking. They were loud and obnoxious, talking over each other. *They probably can't even hear what one another's saying,* I thought, irritably. For the life of me, I couldn't understand why Bri was hanging around her. Mara was just so dreadful. But then so was Bri too, maybe?

I'd read everything I could online about the Landry murders, but there hadn't been as much as I'd expected. Rumor had it that the bodies were found right here, stacked in the dining room. But there were other variations of the story too, versions that included the dead children and wife being tucked neatly into their individual beds, blood staining their covers, or stacked outside in some sort of outbuilding.

Next, I entered the kitchen and went straight to the pantry doors. I'd read everything I could on the construction of old houses, and the pantries were pretty unique on some of these old estates.

I found the pantry door entrance, tucked between the industrial-sized freezer and laundry room space. I slipped inside it, feeling around for a light switch or string, but found none.

I waited for my eyes to adjust to the murky darkness, fingers inspecting each shelf carefully. There were so many boxes and canned goods, and despite my curiosity, I was put off by the musty, mildewy smell inside the cramped space.

Finally, blinking through the dark, my fingers settled on the object I'd been looking for. Heart hammering in my chest, I wrapped my hands around the cold brass knob hidden between the pantry shelves.

Chapter Seventeen

ELIZABETH

The mother-in-law

The stress and tension I'd felt for weeks rolled off me like exhaust fumes; my skin felt soft and dewy, my shoulder blades and lower back melty like grass-fed butter. I'd experienced many things in my seventy-five years of life, but I'd never had a massage before.

I didn't know what I was missing.

I cinched the belt of my robe tighter, head still tingling from the glass of champagne and strawberries the masseuse had offered me during the massage. My stomach rumbled as I made my way through the kitchen and shimmied up to the refrigerator.

There were nearly a dozen unopened bottles of wine

tucked in the double doors. I thought twice about it, reaching for a pitcher of a tea, but then I thought: *To heck with it! You only live once, Elizabeth. And with the way things are going, you don't have much time left on this Earth, anyway.*

Selecting a chilled bottle of Pinot Noir, I set it on the sleek quartz countertop. Opening drawers and cabinets, I searched aimlessly for a wine opener. *Ah. The pantry!*

I had the slick, cold bottle in one hand and with the other, I reached for the pantry door. That's when the door flung open on its own, an eerie white phantom charging toward me.

The bottle slipped from my hand as I stumbled back, shattering on the marble floor. I gasped as the icy cold liquor splashed down my legs.

"Oh, my god. I'm so sorry, Elizabeth! I didn't mean to give you a fright." It was that ghoulish girl Tinsley, dressed all in white with that shock of white hair. She dropped to the floor, scrambling to pick up the pieces of jagged glass. I managed to collect myself and rummaged under the sink for a handful of cleaning towels.

"What on earth were you doing hiding in the pantry?" I asked, thrusting the bunch of towels at her.

She grabbed them, juggling the bunch, and gave me a startled look.

"Sorry. I-I was just looking around. I like old houses … and architecture."

I shook my head, putting a hand to my chest. She truly had given me a fright. For a moment, I'd almost believed that she was some sort of angry poltergeist bursting out of the pantry wall.

"But the door was closed and … and the light's out in there," I said, glancing at the open pantry space behind where she was bent down on the floor, wiping up the perfectly good wine and glass shards.

Tinsley glanced back over her shoulder, to where I was looking. *Why is she so weird?* I wondered, angrily. The tension in my shoulders was back, the desire to drink and be merry all but gone.

"Yeah, I know. I was trying to find the light switch but couldn't."

I frowned, watching the girl swirl and swipe, uselessly smearing the mess around on the floor. I thought about how long I'd been standing in the kitchen, thinking about how great I felt. And how long I'd wandered around, looking for that corkscrew. There was no way she was simply standing in the pantry in the dark with the door closed, looking around for a light, for all that length of time. Perhaps she was a drug user, sneaking in the pantry to shoot up or something. I considered her warily. This generation had no morals or values anymore, so I wouldn't be surprised...

I thought about calling Tinsley out on the lie but arguing with the strange young woman seemed like a big fat waste of my time. We were going out for drinks and dinner in an hour, and I needed to take a nice long shower and change.

"Well, I'll see you later," I said, leaving the girl to clean up the mess she had caused.

Chapter Eighteen

MARA

The best friend

After confirming our dinner reservations, I joined Bri and Georgia in the sunroom. The masseuses were folding up their massage tables and putting away their oils and linens. The whole room smelled calm, like lavender and eucalyptus.

Georgia looked great—rested, fit, and stunning as usual—especially considering all that wheezing and throat rasping from the previous night. The only evidence of her recent reaction was her slightly swollen lips. They were puckered and plump, like two ripe plums on her face. Typical of that bitch to look *better* after suffering from a severe allergic reaction.

She had her phone poised in front of her face, taking a

selfie of herself and Bri. I didn't offer to take the picture for them, and they didn't invite me to join them either.

It was not until the masseuse with the big Dolly Parton hair approached, that I remembered I hadn't fully paid them. I remembered now that it was half down at the time of booking and half on the day of their services. Shit. I needed to find Tinsley.

As the masseuse stood around, awkwardly waiting for payment, I felt my heart rate rising. I didn't have the money to pay her, or anyone today. Not after the debacle with my bank account and all those fraudulent charges.

I owed Tinsley a shitload of money, but she would just have to wait a while.

"If you could give me a minute, I'll go fetch my wallet so I can pay you. Thanks again for coming," I told the blond masseuse. I smiled sheepishly over at her partner, who was hanging back, arms loaded down with the heavy folding tables they'd brought.

I was halfway up the bedroom stairs, when Rosalee emerged on the landing. Gasping, I brought my hands to my mouth, completely surprised by her new look but trying not to show the full shock of it on my face.

The dress Bri and I had picked out in the market was stunning on her, hugging all the right curves and accentuating her best features. The colors looked vibrant against her honeydew complexion and the soft golds and shimmery grays of the makeup complemented the color of her bold, green eyes and thick, dark brows.

"You look incredible, Rosie Poo," I told her, stepping aside so she could waltz down the stairs, showing off her look to the others.

Georgia wolf-whistled and even Bri smiled.

"You look so pretty, Rosalee. You always do," Georgia said.

"Thank you. I feel... great," Rosalee said softly, looking mildly embarrassed by the attention. Her dark hair was curled in loose, beachy waves and LeeAnn had even braided a few pieces of it, giving her a soft, bohemian princess vibe I'd never seen on her before. I'd rarely seen Rosalee wear makeup, or if she did, it was very little.

The new look truly suited her, and I gave myself a mental pat on the back for forcing Tinsley to pay for the makeup artist's services. Rosalee was always beautiful, but now she truly shone, a glow-from-within on display for everyone to see.

I felt a flicker of guilt, for betraying my best friend last night at the poolside, when I spoke about her with Bri. We had joked around, even laughing a bit about the whole maternity clothes debacle. I'd been drawn to Bri, with her drinking and confidence—being around her made me feel like I was in college, partying in my dorm, again. But I'd let down my guard and been less than a loyal bestie to Rosalee, laughing at her expense with her future sister-in-law…

From the corner of my eye, I could see the masseuse still shifting her hips, impatiently. Shit. The money.

After Rosalee spun around, showing off the fabric of her dress to Georgia, I asked, "Did anyone happen to see Tinsley upstairs? I think she was going to pay the second part of the massage fees…"

Rosalee stopped turning and gave me a curious look. "No, I haven't seen her for a while. No one else was upstairs but us."

"Huh." Tinsley was probably skulking around or hiding away somewhere reading those strange books of hers. "I guess I'd better go and look for her," I said, offering another apologetic half-smile to the masseuse.

"No worries. I got it," Bri said, giving me a curt stare. "Do you take PayPal, Zelle, or Venmo?" I heard her asking the masseuse.

Thank god.

I took Rosalee's hand in mine as Bri handled the payment for me.,. My finances were a disaster, and until I got to the bottom of who had hacked my account and stolen my funds I was unable to pay for anything.

I squeezed Rosalee's hand. "You always look lovely, Rosalee, but tonight, you look simply ravishing. Are you ready for a night on the town … dinner… dancing?" I lifted her hand, and brushed it with a goofy kiss while trying to push away my guilt for betraying her; my concern over the creditors who were waiting back home to beat down my door played on my mind.

Rosalee giggled. "Ready as I'll ever be, I suppose," she said.

Chapter Nineteen

GEORGIA

The groom's friend

The sidewalk in front of Deanie's restaurant was lined with people waiting to enter. Through the big front windows, I could see that nearly every table was full.

"Good thing I thought to make a reservation," Mara said, zigzagging through the queue of waiting patrons and motioning for us to follow her through the front door.

"This place doesn't look very fancy," I heard Elizabeth moaning behind me. She had been quiet since our talk by the pool this morning; the silence between us during the massages grew so uncomfortable, that I'd been forced to pretend I was sleeping just to escape it.

"Table for six under the name of Mattingly, please," Mara told the white-collared woman who was at the hostess stand ticking off names.

"Right this way," she said, and led our group past a brightly colored bar crammed with happy, chatting diners, to a large booth towards the back of the restaurant.

I was grateful for the privacy as, despite the massage, I could feel a migraine coming on; the fluorescent lights in the room causing a sharp, throbbing pain in my eyes and temples. I took a seat at the end of the table, far away from Elizabeth. As we all sat, I watched her take her white napkin and place it daintily in her lap. I tried to catch her eye, but she refused to meet my gaze. She was still angry and bitter from earlier at the poolside.

I loved Asher. There was no doubt about that. But I didn't love him in the way that Elizabeth wanted or needed me to.

Love is easy to come by, in my opinion. But friendship—good, real, true companionship—regardless of gender—is so scarce that some people spend their whole lives living without it. There are friends and acquaintances, people we meet throughout our lives—sharing interests, activities, or common goals. But true kinship, the ability to love someone for who they are, is a rarity. When I was younger, I just took it for granted and didn't realize that my childhood friendship with Asher would be the only real one of its kind; I had dozens of other friends after him, but none of those were the same. Not the kind of friendship where you can disappear for a year and come back and pick right up where you left off; souls connecting like they never parted in the first place.

It seemed silly to describe my relationship with Asher in this way. So, I could see why Elizabeth thought it was love—the lovey-dovey kind of love—but she couldn't have been more wrong.

You see, people don't feel sorry for kids like me and Asher. We grew up with rich parents and entitlements that most kids could only dream of. But we were lonely… painfully lonely, all we had was each other. I had no siblings, and Asher was never particularly close to Bri, not until they got older. Bri was a whiz kid, always going off to special schools or science camps, so I fulfilled the role of his sister most days. And he certainly was a brother in mine.

While our parents spent their evenings and weekends at parties, Asher and I were often dragged along for the ride. The only kids in an adult-centered world, we were unseen and unheard, money or toys shoved in our hands to distract us. So, instead we distracted each other.

We became best friends at such a young age, at a time when sex and puberty and gender weren't even a factor. We didn't know or understand those things; all we knew was that we were pals, one minute playing pirates and the next minute playing house. We shared all our secrets and kept each other company, otherwise we would have died of loneliness or boredom back then.

By the time hormones kicked in, it was already too late to consider anything more than friendship. By that point, the thought of treating Asher as more than a friend made me nauseous, and he admitted that he felt the same. He confided in me when he developed crushes on girls at school, and I did the same with him. One of my worst-favorite memories with Asher was when we attended Kelly Maynard's birthday party together. Such an event was a rarity, we weren't used to being around other kids much, and certainly not in social situations; we were both hyped up and looking forward to it. There was a Snoopy snow cone machine at the party which Kelly was pissed about, as she had wanted some sort of ice cream maker instead. But Asher and I loved it. The crank was hard to turn, so I loaded the ice and Asher crushed it for me, leaning on the crank while I captured the blue-dyed icy treat in my miniature cup.

I drank so many of those tiny cups that by the end of the party, the pain in my stomach was excruciating. I tried to make it to the bathroom in time but failed. Diarrhea leaked through the bottom of my neatly pressed trousers and dribbled on my clean white shoes. Asher rushed to my aid, trying to clean me up with thin paper party napkins. The kids never forgot it, chanting,

"Georgia Britt smells like shit" in the hallways and telling everyone who would listen that Asher was my personal toilet paper man. It was so stupid, such a childish thing. But looking back at the way all those boys and girls who called themselves friends laughed at me, and the way Asher rushed to my aid, hecklers be damned. It wasn't necessarily a fond memory, but it solidified our friendship and Asher's loyalty to me.

I'd told Elizabeth the truth today, even though she didn't want to hear it. Yes, I loved her son. But I'd never love him in the way Rosalee loved him, or the way Elizabeth wished and hoped I would. Asher and I would always be friends, the best of friends. But nothing more than that...

By the time the waiter came around to our table, I was still unsure what to order. When he suggested the shrimp and onion ring basket, I agreed and closed my menu.

"Just make sure it's not coconut shrimp. She's allergic," Rosalee said, touching the waiter's elbow. I gave her a small, grateful smile, and looked over at Mara. She was always watching, always analyzing my every move, it seemed. Once again, I couldn't shake off the feeling that she'd been the one responsible for organizing the caterers to prepare the coconut cake.. For the rest of the weekend, I'd have to be careful. For more reasons than just the silly, overprotective likes of Mara.

· · ·

Despite the buzzing crowds at the restaurant, our food arrived in record time. We had all ordered fried food, and Rosalee had asked for a round of beers for us all. I hadn't realized she was a beer drinker, but it made sense—Asher loved cheap beer, too. I smiled, imagining the two of them at home together on the weekends, drinking beer and watching baseball. Asher had never been the sporty kid his parents wanted him to be; he liked watching and cheering, but he had hated playing.

"Cheers to all of you," Rosalee said, lifting her bottle. I clinked mine to hers, then reached across the table to touch Tinsley's bottle too. Tinsley had been quiet all evening, but she seemed to be quiet in general so perhaps that was the norm for her.

"Yes, cheers," Elizabeth said, mouth droopy at the corners. I hadn't realized she was buzzed already, but then remembered the champagne the masseuse had offered her earlier.

"To a long and happy marriage with my son. Welcome to our family. I can't think of a better daughter," Elizabeth said, smiling broadly at Rosalee.

Rosalee looked stunned, mouth dropping momentarily, before she collected herself and replied, "Thank you so much, Elizabeth."

Elizabeth didn't look at me when she said those words, but I knew she'd said them to take a sneaky dig at

Bri and me. If she thought being kind to Asher's future bride would hurt my feelings, she was sorely mistaken.

I glanced over at Bri, wincing when I saw the painful look on her face.

"Hear, hear!" I said, lifting the bottle to my lips and chugging half of it down in one long swig. I hadn't had an ice-cold beer in so long—not only did it taste good but it was a welcome distraction from Elizabeth's anger and the feeling that, at the moment, everyone seemed to want me dead. .

It was mostly all smiles around the table as we dipped our greasy seafood and sides in ketchup and chatted about nothing, and everything. I lifted my phone, using the camera to take several quick photos of the candid moments for my Instagram feed. *Now, that is the perfect group photo*, I thought, the edges of the room blurring as the beer kicked in, warming up my belly.

I swiped back and forth through the recent photos, trying to decide which one was best. And that's when I noticed a table of men in the background of the photo, one of them staring at us intensely.

I sat the phone down on the table and glanced over towards the table. He was still there, and still watching us. He saw me looking towards him and his lips parted baring locked teeth in a wolfish grin. It was the kind of smile that seemed less friendly, and more predatory—the kind of smile every woman knows and has felt before at some time in their lives...

Why was he watching us? He was giving me the creeps; could he be related to the violent, threatening messages I'd been receiving?

My stomach twisted in knots as I pushed my dish back and excused myself for the bathroom. Both my appetite and euphoria from earlier all but forgotten.

Chapter Twenty

ROSALEE

The bride-to-be

Bourbon Street was already buzzing with music and happy voices as we followed the cracked sidewalks, smiling and nodding at the friendly passers-by. We could hear it before we saw it, a celebration that never ended, or so it seemed; dancers stomped their feet and clapped their hands in the street and buskers played on the corners. Music flowed from hidden courtyards and side streets: jazzy blues tones pouring through the open door of one bar, soulful gospel sung in unison from a nightclub balcony of another. It was a diverse and colorful crowd dressed in bright clothing, some wearing costumes or face paint. Two women roamed the streets on massive stilts, their nipples covered with only thin pasties.

"It's hard to know if this is heaven or hell," I said, looking at Tinsley with a forced smile.

"A little bit of both, perhaps," she said, nudging me gently with her elbow as we strolled along Bourbon Street, jostling with the crowds.

The streets had a unique smell to them which I couldn't place—something lemony, but old and woody too and of spilled liquor and fried foods.

"Can you imagine how crowded it must be during Mardi Gras?" Georgia asked, looking around at the hordes of people. There was something in her demeanor I hadn't noticed before—a nervousness I would never have expected from someone who spent so much of their time in front of others doing yoga or showing off her daily life online.

The crowds seemed friendly, party-goers throwing brightly colored beads from the wrought-iron balconies, and men handing out roses, blood red and perfect.

"Yeah, this is nothing compared to Mardi Gras. You're packed in like a sardine then," Tinsley said.

"You've been before? I didn't realize you'd been to New Orleans," I said, looking at my cousin. There were so many things I didn't know about her life now; we'd grown so far apart over the last few years.

"Yeah. You were in college. I came with a few girls I

worked with at the bookstore. They've all moved on to other jobs now… but it was fun, I guess. I didn't get along too well with them, but I made my own way and enjoyed the festivities. I wish you had been there with me. It would have been more fun, like this," Tinsley said. I reached for her hand, and she took it easily.

"We're here now, and that's all that matters," I told her.

Elizabeth looked overwhelmed and tipsy as she leaned on Bri, but she was trying to be a good sport, it seemed. Mara led us to a bluesy bar that featured live music and quickly found us a couple of small wooden tables near the dance floor. She ordered a round of shots and glasses of Scotch.

It seemed like a bad idea, mixing all these different types of alcohol together. But it was, after all, a celebration, and I was determined to have a good time.

The shots arrived first, followed by the Scotch. All at once, we downed them together, hissing from the syrupy burn in unison. Even Elizabeth finished her shot, knocking her tiny glass on the table when she was done.

She had chosen a seat next to me again, and I couldn't help wondering what had changed with her. She seemed more distant from Georgia than she had before, and I'd be lying if I said that it didn't make me feel good to have more of her attention on me. And Georgia seemed unusually skittish, her eyes roaming the bar, distractedly.

The band was loud, the powerful sound of the saxophone and trumpets blaring in the cramped nightclub. Feet thumped to the rhythm of the music causing the wooden dance floor to vibrate. The area was filling up fast, guests swinging their arms and legs wildly to the growing beat.

After a few more drinks, Mara had cajoled all of us onto our feet, and led us to the dance floor. She pushed her way through the crowd, clearing a space in the center for the six of us. The room was spinning, the music vibrating my very soul, and although I wasn't normally much of a dancer, I found my body swaying side to side with the other people in the crowd, the smile on my face so wide it was stretching at the corners of my mouth. Although I wasn't normally one for makeup and fancy clothes, I felt beautiful after having my makeover.

"Take some pictures of me while I look hot!" I shouted, pointing over at Georgia, who was now staring down at her phone with a tight, pained look. She looked lost for a moment, staring blankly over at me, but then she nodded, lifting her phone to snap more pics.

As I turned on the dance floor, moving my hips, I was surprised to find Elizabeth with her eyes closed, face tilted to the ceiling above. She was rocking her body from side to side, clutching her cold glass of Scotch to her chest. When she opened her eyes and caught me looking, she flashed me with the most genuine smile I'd ever received from her.

"Edmund would have loved this music!" she shouted over the noise. "He was such a sucker for soul music."

"I wish he was here right now," I told her, truthfully.

It felt like just moments later that I found myself leaning on Bri and Mara, both of them propping me up from behind. I was so tipsy I could barely walk. At first, I thought they were leading me away from the bar and Bourbon Street, but then I discovered I was in a new club. This one had a band front and center too, and they were playing cover songs.

"I love this song!" I cheered, mouthing the melancholic lyrics to "Something in the Way" by Nirvana. It was one of those songs that was perfect for sad, hormone-riddled teens—Tinsley and I had played it over and over in her mom's car and in our room at night.

"I know you do," Tinsley said, mouth close to my ear. "I'm going to go get you a water."

"Okay!" I shouted, letting Bri guide me over to a long booth near the back of the bar. Out of all of us, she seemed the most sober. *Did the beers, bourbon, and shots have no effect on her?* I wondered, incredulously. When Tinsley returned with my water, I took large gulps, enjoying the icy cold freshness of it. I'd never tasted anything so good.

Even from the back of the room, the music found

me, its rhythm reaching like long, skinny fingers through the crowd, vibrating my chest and filling my heart with a silly flutter of glee. I hadn't felt this kind of rush since college. The floor beneath my feet was stretching, the crevices in the wood swirling like tiny rivers of rust.

"Drink up. You look like you're going to keel over," Tinsley told me, lifting the water glass to my lips and encouraging me to drink some more.

It didn't take long for the water to work, sobering me up just enough to realize that Elizabeth was ready to leave. She looked exhausted and even drunker than I was, limbs heavy and eyes drooping, slouched over the table.

My blurry eyes moved from one lady to the next, taking in all of my friends' faces. Georgia was still on her phone—texting Asher? My rush of joy was quickly replaced with paranoia. I had a sudden impulse to yank that phone right out of her hands. Was she having an affair with my fiancé? Who had been sending her weird threats, any why?

I looked around for the one face that always comforted me, and spotted Tinsley ducking down near a table by Georgia. What the hell was she doing? Tinsley was staring at someone across the room—I followed her gaze and saw a group of men staring at her. Not just her, our entire group.

"What is it, Tinsley? What's wrong?" I shouted over the music.

She stood up straighter, looking embarrassed.

"It's nothing. Just some creepy guy who drove the taxi I arrived in. He and a group of his friends are watching us."

This seemed to catch Georgia's attention. She tucked her phone away and followed to where Tinsley was trying to point without being too obvious about it.

"I saw him, too! In the restaurant earlier. I think they've been following us!"

I rolled my eyes. This whole thing seemed a little dramatic.

"Just because they're checking us out and they went to the same club and restaurant we did, doesn't mean they're predators."

Georgia and Tinsley both shot me an irritated look. I put up my hands in retreat. *My bad.*

"I think it's probably about time to go," I said, but no one seemed to be listening. Tinsley, Georgia, and Mara were focused on the leering group of men and… Where were Elizabeth and Bri?

Finally, I spotted them, standing near the bar. Bri was ordering another drink and I could tell by the looks on both women's faces that they were arguing. Was Elizabeth nagging her about her drinking again?

I walked toward them, thinking of ordering another

water. Before I even got close enough for them to see me, I could hear their words. It wasn't Elizabeth who was angry and disgusted this time; it was Bri.

"Did you think Asher and I were going to be okay with this? How dare you try to hide it for so long? It's such a bitch move," Bri snarled at her mother. Elizabeth looked taken aback, eyes widening as she swayed side to side on her feet.

Through the crowds, I looked back and finally was able to catch Tinsley's eye. We had always been good at reading each other's lips.

We have to get out of here now. Please. I mouthed the words. She nodded and took out her phone.

"Sorry to interrupt, but I'm ready to go back now. The cab will be here in a few minutes," I said to Bri and Elizabeth, taking Elizabeth's arm in mine. Bri turned away; their argument instantly silenced at the sight of me.

Bri accepted a shot from the bartender and threw it back. "Fine by me. Get me the hell out of here," she said, side-eyeing her mom once more.

Mara tried to insist on visiting a few more bars, but Tinsley had already ordered the cab. After we had settled our bills, we stood outside waiting until finally, our cab turned up. I wanted nothing more than to get back to the mansion, wrap myself in my thick, fluffy robe, and stretch out like a princess in that four-poster bed.

Everyone's jolly moods had dissipated quickly, but I was still feeling the perfect blend of euphoria and control.

Perhaps when I got back to my room at the mansion, I would take some naked pictures of myself with all my makeup and fancy hair and send them to Asher. A little drunk sexting from across the country with the man of my dreams sounded pretty fun. I was usually too shy for that sort of thing, but I knew Asher would like it, and the liquid courage I was feeling made me feel like a whole new person.

Chapter Twenty-One

MARA

The best friend

The house seemed like it was waiting for us, lit up like a big, glowing jack-o-lantern in the dark when the cab pulled up the drive of the Leblanc-Landry estate. Tinsley assumed I was stupid, and that I didn't know the gruesome history of this place. But, perhaps, that was part of the appeal for me.

Turn something dark and ugly into something beautiful and bright. The mansion had come with a heavy discount because of its sordid past. If I'd known from the beginning that I could get Tinsley to foot the entire bill, I would have chosen somewhere even more luxurious to stay.

Every last one of us was drunk, but Bri and I seemed

to be holding our own. We both had more experience with alcohol than the others, the night's festivities on Bourbon only kicking off when the others were already ready to leave.

The long, traffic-filled ride back to the mansion had given everyone a bit of time to sober up. I needed them alert so they could enjoy my next bit of fun.

"No one can go to bed yet!" I declared as we walked through the French doors. "Out to the courtyard first," I told them, motioning the drunken herd to follow me.

"I'm tired, Mara. I'm not in the mood for swimming," Bri said, tripping over her own feet and dumping out half the contents of her purse on the floor. Several pill bottles rattled on the ground, and she bent down quickly to scoop them up.

I guess the pill-popper is going to be a party pooper, too, I thought, wearily.

We moved through the dining room, and I gasped at the trays of appetizers the caterers had left out for us, along with nearly a dozen bottles of wine. Oysters, hush puppies, miniature po-boy sandwiches, and barbeque shrimp were laid out on trays for us to snack on. I'd arranged for them earlier in the evening; they were probably cold by now. Honestly, I'd forgotten all about the amount of food I'd ordered. I'd requested so many things for the party—perhaps I did go a little overboard on Tinsley's dime…

I scooped up a sandwich, but the others groaned at the food, disinterested in more indulgences.

"Don't worry. We're not going swimming," I told Bri, my mouth still full of food. "There's a little fire pit out there in the courtyard and I was going to light a fire for us."

"It's too hot for a fire, Mara," Georgia said, clutching her Elizabeth's arm in earnest. Elizabeth looked the worst for wear. She probably could have used Georgia in that moment for a prop, but she yanked her arm away, giving Georgia a disgusted frown.

Wow. Their little bond fizzled out quickly, I thought, wincing.

"The fire isn't for the heat, it's for atmosphere. I thought we could tell some ghost stories or something. Or have a final girls' powwow on our last night together in the mansion. We can't end it in a drunken stupor, ladies!" I said, trying to muster up some much-needed enthusiasm.

They were all about to shut me down again, but then Rosalee belched and said, "I love bonfires! Let's do it. I'm feeling re-energized!"

It had been so long since I'd seen her drunk, not since our early days in college. She was more fun this way, and more pliable too.

"Yes! The guest of honor gets to do what she wants!" I exclaimed, giving the others a triumphant look.

Everyone shuffled into the courtyard, and I set to work stacking the logs in a perfect formation, using lighter fluid to get the flame going quickly. Bri helped me tug chairs around the pit, and the six of us took our seats around the fire, eyes glowing as we watched shadows dancing over our faces through the flames.

We looked like bright pumpkins, shadows lengthening and faces ghastly in the orange, florid light.

"I know! Instead of stories, we should play truth or dare. Remember when we used to play that, Tinsley?" Rosalee pointed across the circle at her cousin.

I groaned. "What are we, in third grade?"

Tinsley gave me a dirty look, then smiled and nodded at Rosalee.

"Yes, truth or dare! I have a question," Elizabeth blurted out of nowhere, shocking the hell out of me. "What's going on between you two?" She pointed a finger at me, then motioned over to Tinsley.

"That's not quite how the game works, Elizabeth. First, you have to ask one another truth or dare," I said, rolling my eyes at the obnoxious, know-it-all woman. Even though she was sitting, she was practically draped over Bri's lap, clearly still drunk.

I tried to catch Bri's eye for back-up, but she was unusually quiet tonight and had been for hours. Perhaps she was simply too drunk and messed up on all those pills I saw in her purse.

"That's okay. You can ask me about it," Tinsley piped up, scooting forward in her chair, shimmying up to the flames. Unlike the others, it struck me for the first time that she looked stone-cold sober. "I choose truth, Elizabeth. So, I'll tell you," Tinsley said, with her self-satisfied grin. This was what Tinsley had been waiting for all weekend. *A chance to expose me, to get back at me for screwing her out of so much money*, I thought, angrily.

"There's nothing to tell," I said, poking a stick I'd found earlier in the nearby shrubbery at the crackling pit of flames. *Just shut up, bitch*, I wanted to scream at Tinsley. As much as Rosalee cared for her, I couldn't understand why. She was strange and rude. Not to mention dull.

"Oh, there is plenty to tell," Tinsley said. "You see, ladies, Mara did most of the planning for this party. But she hasn't paid a single dime for any of it. Apparently, she's having some serious money troubles. And I can't help feeling taken advantage of. So, that's what the tension is about. I've racked up a mountain of debt in order to meet her ridiculous demands for this weekend. And she isn't even the least bit sorry. Sounds to me like she's grown accustomed to taking advantage of others. Thanks for the question." Tinsley shot Elizabeth a quick smile, then sat back in her chair and crossed her arms, looking rather pleased with herself.

"Tinsley, I didn't know that," Rosalee said, shooting a

worried glance at me. "I didn't want you all to do this much for me. I never would have let you do this if I'd have known you'd have to pay for all of it. I know you can't afford that…"

"And how would you know, Rosalee? You always make assumptions about my life. That I'm poor and broke, just because I didn't go to college. Just because I'm not like you doesn't mean I can't be successful," Tinsley snapped.

"Whoa." I could feel the sting of her words. As bad as I felt for Rosalee and her crumpling face, I was glad to have the heat off me and my money problems for a brief moment.

"That's not what I meant. I just didn't want you to have to pay for everything…" Rosalee raised her eyebrows at me, waiting for me to explain myself. But there was no way I could tell her the truth.

"Truth or dare, Georgia," I interrupted.

Georgia looked like she was caught in the headlights, shell-shocked and leery. I couldn't blame her.

Georgia poked out her chin. "Dare," she said, firmly.

I leaned back and crossed my arms, visibly disappointed. I'd wanted to grill her with questions about Asher. But she probably wouldn't have told the truth anyway.

"I dare you to get lost. Go inside and take a bath and put yourself to bed. You don't belong here anyway. You barely even know Rosalee," I said, voice laced with the venom I felt.

Georgia surprised me with a loud, abrupt chuckle. Then she curled her lips and narrowed her eyes. "Fuck you, bitch," she said, boldly, "and the horse you rode in on. You don't know anything about me, but that didn't stop you from trying to kill me last night! I told you three separate times in our group emails that I was allergic to coconut."

I shrugged. "Must have missed that one," I said.

"Must have," Georgia said. "I'll gladly 'get lost', Mara. But not until you tell the truth. Why did you give me coconut on purpose, huh? What if it had killed me? Who put you up to it, huh?"

I swallowed, my short-lived bravado wearing thin as I scanned the other faces—everyone looked sickened by me. *Well, join the club, people. Sometimes I even disgust myself with my own choices and actions.*

"No one put me up to it, Georgia. You are just paranoid. It was a joke. I didn't mean to hurt you, and that's the truth."

"So, it was deliberate! How dare you?" Rosalee said, squinting at me in the dark. "You don't need to go anywhere, Georgia. I'm sure Mara didn't mean it, and I want you here. You belong here."

I groaned at my oldest friend. Always the people-pleaser! "What a joke! Why don't you tell everyone about the anonymous notes in your basket, Rosie-Poo? Who do you think wrote the one about keeping Asher sexually satisfied? You and I both know it was her." I pointed a finger across the flames at Georgia, the fire singeing the tip of my finger.

"How do you know what the notes said, Mara? I didn't tell you about them." Rosalee pushed her chair back and stood. If looks could kill, I'd be dead already.

"Because I'm the one who handed you the basket, remember? Everyone sent me their well wishes in envelopes before the party, I just loaded them into the basket and decorated it for you..."

"But you had to look, right? Had to read them for yourself?" Tinsley said, looking wickedly satisfied to see everyone turning on me.

"Of course I read them beforehand," I said, with a shrug.

"So, you knew about the mean notes, and you just sat there urging me on to read them... You knew how I would react. A true friend would have warned me or taken the notes out!" Rosalee cried.

"I don't know what you're talking about exactly, but it sounds like it would have been pretty easy for Mara to write those mean words herself," Elizabeth said, with a hard expression. "Believe me, Georgia isn't sleeping with my son. She thinks she's too good for that!"

Georgia gaped at Elizabeth, and I laughed at this

interesting turn of events. So, Georgia wasn't Elizabeth's favorite anymore? I must have missed something between those two, I realized.

I turned to Rosalee, but she would barely look at me, still standing over the flames with a furious expression on her face.

"It wasn't me. It was probably her, trying to stir up trouble," I said, pointing at Elizabeth. Now, it was her turn to gape at me.

"Rosalee told me what a bitch you are, Elizabeth," I said. "You and your stupid passive aggressive Christmas gifts and always treating Rosalee like shit."

I stood up to face Rosalee across the flames. "I'm the only one here who actually has your back here, don't you see that?" I said, reaching across the fire for her hand. She yanked away from me and stepped away from the fire.

"I don't see that, Mara! In fact, I don't really trust a single one of you," Rosalee said, bitterly, looking around the circle at each of us.

And with that, the guest of honor stormed off, leaving the five of us sitting in silence, dealing with the aftermath of our hideous party.

Chapter Twenty-Two

THE AFTERMATH

The heavy winds arrive just after midnight, blowing from the north, reversing waterways and creating strong gusts that threatened to morph into cyclones.

None of the six guests are asleep, unable to settle down after the way it all ended. They were joyous and happy at the outset, but those worms were digging through the soil, working overtime to disassemble the already fragile bonds that had formed between them.

The guest of honor is taking a bath. The water is scorching, punishing her red, raw skin and making it raging hot, just like her mood. None of the women are truly her friends, she realizes. None of them can be trusted.

The mother-in-law is changing, tugging off her stiff

daily garments and pulling on her still-damp bathing suit. She isn't afraid to swim in a thunderstorm. She is ready to make peace with death. She feels it knocking daily.

The sister-in-law is angry, pacing the floor of her room. Her anger booms inside her chest, harder than the thunder. And much more powerful.

The cousin does what she always does when she is anxious. She reaches for the one thing she loves and knows—literature. The windows of the house rattle in their frames as she leaves her room, carrying her book. Shortly after, the power goes out.

The groom's friend is crying in the dark. She forces herself to read all the messages on her phone before the battery dies out completely. Every angry line and every threat. She knows she deserves what is coming. After all, she's responsible for taking a life.

The best friend is drinking, taking long pulls from a bottle of tequila she found in the kitchen cupboard earlier. It's the kind of tequila that has a worm in the bottom of the bottle. She wonders what would happen if she drank it all, swallowed that ghastly creature whole. Maybe she would transform into something better, someone resembling a human being, not this wasteful shell she's been stuck in.

All the ladies are stewing separately, not realizing that they will soon be brought back together with a death…

Part Two

~

"Keep quiet and the enemy will reveal himself."

— *Bangambiki Habyarimana*

Chapter Twenty-Three

INTERVIEW: SUSPECT #1

Detective Nina Smalls wasn't what anyone would consider 'old', but she had been around the block a time or two, as her father used to say. She grew up as the daughter of a prominent beat cop, who was eventually promoted to detective and retired as the head police chief just as his daughter joined the academy.

She was eight years old when she attended her very first crime scene. Strangely enough, that day also happened to be her birthday. Detective Rod Smalls had promised her a birthday cake with police cars on top of it and a trip to the arcade. He had managed to get her the cake but the trip to the arcade was thwarted by an emergency call.

As a single father, finding last-minute babysitters wasn't an easy feat. And he couldn't leave his precious

Nina on her birthday... but duty called. Family, duty, community, and honor. The four most important pillars in life, according to him.

"Take me with you," she had begged.

Detective Rod Smalls knew it was wrong, but he didn't have much of a choice. Sometimes choosing between his four pillars was hard—he loved his daughter, but he also had a responsibility to his community. He had to keep all of them safe, or at least work to right the wrongs when he failed to do so.

When he arrived at the scene of a recent shootout, he had instructed one of his deputies to keep an eye on Nina. *Don't move. Stay right here,* he had ordered.

But Detective Rod Smalls should have known better. His daughter listened about as well as he did when it came to prioritizing her safety over others.

Nina had raced through the legs of his deputy, zigzagged through a stream of personnel, and entered the crime scene at her father's heels.

There were blood and bullet holes everywhere, but no body. No known killer, no obvious victims. Just a big messy scene.

If her father had been surprised to see her there, he didn't show it. His eyes were roving the carpets and walls, pinpointing bullet holes and casings.

"Every crime scene tells a story," he told her, his voice eerily soft in the already quiet room. "But unlike a story you read in books or watch on TV, you usually only have one real chance to get it right. The scene isn't the same the second or third time… You must see it all. Every last detail. And don't let anyone tell you that law enforcement is all analytics and methodical working. It's an art, really. And just like storytellers, we often have to connect the dots using intuition, and sometimes our imagination, as our guide."

It was funny how Detective Nina Smalls—now thirty-nine years old and her father long buried in the ground—couldn't remember what she ate for breakfast yesterday, but she could remember her father's words. She fell in love with policework before the age of eight, but that fateful date with her father at the crime scene… It was the most memorable birthday she ever had. And it solidified her love of policework and her fate to follow in her father's shoes.

Now she sat at a table in an interrogation room, trying to connect the dots of what she knew about Georgia Britt, former nurse and yoga extraordinaire.

"It was an accident," Georgia said, face resting in her palms.

"An accident," Detective Smalls parroted back to her. It was another tactic she learned from her father, and one often used by therapists to demonstrate they are listening to clients and want them to further clarify or explore their own words. Strangely, Detective Smalls had found her psychology training to be more useful than most of the law enforcement exercises from the academy.

"I never meant to… I would never hurt someone on purpose," Georgia said.

"And by someone… are we talking about Brian Massey?" Detective Smalls pressed.

Georgia shrunk down farther in her chair, suddenly looking less like a tall, athletic, fitness guru, and more like a lost little girl.

"Yes. I'd been out of nursing school for less than a year when it happened. I was so happy, so excited… well, not that any of that matters. I fucked up, okay?"

"You fucked up?"

"Well, you obviously already looked into it and know what happened. Brian Massey beat cancer. The kid was a god damn warrior. But the doctors recommended one last round of chemo, just to be sure. Poor kid beats the odds and kicks cancer's ass, only to be murdered by a stupid newbie nurse who couldn't do simple math."

"Do you really think you murdered him, Georgia?" Detective Smalls asked, her voice softening.

"What does how I feel about Brian Massey have to do with this?" Georgia looked into the eyes of the detective, the first note of challenge in her voice. "And to answer your question, no I didn't murder him. Because murder requires that someone does something on purpose to take another's life. I didn't mean to shoot fifty times over the recommended dose of sodium chloride into his veins, but I did. Accident or not, it was my fault. I was humming as I injected it into the intravenous bag… Can you believe that? Some stupid song, all the while I was killing a little boy and ruining his mother's life."

Georgia couldn't hold in the tears any longer; thick sobs rocked her body, shaking the table between them.

"Georgia." Detective Smalls, in an unusual display of affection, reached across the table and put her hand over the suspect's. "Medical errors are something like the third leading cause of death in this country. Did you know that?"

Georgia shook her head and wiped her eyes.

"Not sure how that's supposed to make me feel better, no offense," she said.

"You're right. It won't make it better. Not for you. Not for Brian. Certainly not for his mother. But you're not the first rookie nurse to make a mistake like that, and unfortunately, you won't be the last. What happened to Brian Massey was awful and tragic, but that still doesn't make it okay for Rebecca Massey to stalk you. You were cleared by the medical board," Detective Smalls said.

"Yeah, I was. Asher was my attorney, but the hospital settled the wrongful death suit out of court and I left my job quietly. But that wasn't enough for Brian's mom. She wants to see my head on a stick, and I can't say I blame her. Do you?"

Detective Smalls shrugged. In truth, she understood the mother's fury. She couldn't imagine watching her child nearly die of cancer, only to survive and lose his life over something so stupid. But still… Rebecca Massey had received a settlement and Georgia was cleared. The hundreds of threatening messages on Georgia's phone were not only uncalled for, they also constituted a crime. But that still didn't mean that Rebecca Massey was responsible for last night's murder. She had no reason to come all the way to New Orleans and kill the wrong person.

"Do you think Rebecca had something to do with this? Is that why you're asking?" Georgia asked, eyes widening with realization.

"I don't think so. But we did see all the messages on your phone. The threats and the warnings. I'm surprised you haven't taken out a restraining order against her."

Now it was Georgia's turn to shrug. "She's old and she's hurting. I don't think she actually wants to hurt me. I think she just wants me to constantly be reminded of what I did and what it cost her. But what she doesn't realize is that I'll never forget. I tried to move on and start my own yoga studio but that's failing miserably, and I still think about that sweet little boy every day. I'm so tormented by what I did, and nobody even really knows. The hospital just swept it under the rug the way hospitals do sometimes."

"But Asher knew," Detective Smalls said, raising her eyebrows. "One of the other party guests mentioned your relationship with him, and something about a monthly membership to your gym. He's your friend and attorney. Is he also your lover, Georgia?"

Georgia took a deep breath, then exhaled noisily. Her breath smelled stale from across the table.

"Of course not. Asher and I have been best friends since we were in diapers. Thinking of him in that way is just plain gross. He's always been like a brother to me. And as far as the gym membership goes, that was his stupid idea. I'd insisted on paying him for his attorney services with the Massey hearings. I didn't want to take advantage of his friendship. He deserved to get paid for helping me. It was the least I could do for asking for his legal advice and counsel at the last minute. I forced the money on him, even though he wanted to help me pro bono. When I set up my yoga studio, he was in there the next day, forcing my assistant to sign him up for a monthly membership fee, even though I didn't even have enough clients to set up regular memberships. Asher hates yoga and I knew right away that it was his way of funneling the money back to me. He knew I was headed for financial ruin after being forced out from my nursing job. All that school debt, no one who would hire me, and my new, destined-to-fail business… He was being a good friend, that's all. There's nothing more to it than that. My relationship with Asher has nothing to do with this crime…"

"Rebecca Massey wrote in her texts that she knew where you were, and she was coming. Did she know you were in New Orleans? Had you been in contact with her?" Detective Smalls asked. It was a rhetorical question, really. Nowadays, everyone, including Detective Smalls herself, had at least one social media account. Georgia had accounts on all the major platforms, and most of her updates and photos were public.

"I posted where I was going on Facebook and Instagram. That's how she knew. She likes to troll me relentlessly online, too. If hounding me every day makes her feel better, then it's the price I'll pay. I said before, I don't think she would really do something… Do you think she actually came to New Orleans?" Georgia asked, nervously.

Detective Smalls shook her head. "So far, it looks like she was at home yesterday. Local authorities near her home have spoken with her. It would have been nearly impossible for her to commit a murder and make it all the way back home that fast, but it's something we're definitely looking into at the moment. She certainly seemed angry enough to kill, possibly commit murder. But you seemed to be her only focus and interest."

Georgia flinched at the word 'murder'.

"I made a huge mistake, and I killed a kind, innocent boy who deserved to live a wonderful life. And I'll spend the rest of my days feeling guilty. But I didn't murder anyone, you have to know that. I would never hurt someone intentionally no matter how mad they made me," Georgia cried.

The detective watched the young woman, tears flowing through her fingers, face swollen from crying. Her answers seemed genuine. Believable. She had no real motive to commit this crime, at least not that the detective could see, yet.

"Were you aware that the power went out just after midnight?"

"Yes, I remember," Georgia said, sniffling.

"Where were you when the lights went out?"

"I was in bed, reading those awful messages Rebecca Massey sent me. My phone died and I couldn't charge it because of the outage. So, I rolled over and finally went to sleep. Until... the screams woke me a few hours later."

The detective nodded, still trying to work out her feelings and general impression of Georgia Britt.

Chapter Twenty-Four

INTERVIEW: SUSPECT #2

Unlike Georgia, Elizabeth Beake was a hard one to crack. She sat across the interview table, arms crossed tightly over her chest, looking down her long, patrician nose at Detective Nina Smalls.

"How old are you?" she demanded, eyes beady and hard. Despite what had happened, Elizabeth seemed stoic and tight-lipped. A woman used to being in control.

In some ways, she reminded Detective Nina Smalls of herself. On the outside, Nina looked and felt like a normal person, in control and steady at hand. A professional at all times. But underneath the surface, she was riddled with anxiety and worry, always thinking of her city and all those innocent lives she felt responsible for protecting. So many cases went unsolved, and it was those cases that kept her up at night. She prayed this murder wouldn't be another one of those.

"My age is none of your concern, Ms. Beake, and frankly, it's irrelevant anyway," the detective said. Elizabeth sat back in her chair, shrinking an inch. She was the kind of woman who tested boundaries and adapted accordingly. *If she knows I'm in charge, then perhaps she will change her approach,* the detective thought.

"You're right. I'm sorry. You just look so young. Please, can you tell me what's going on?" Elizabeth said, face morphing into an elderly, desperate woman.

"What's going on is that there's been a murder. Tell me what you know, Ms. Beake. I want to see if what you know matches up with what I know. Understood?"

"Please call me Elizabeth. Ms. Beake makes me feel old."

"Okay, Elizabeth. Tell me what you know about the murder," Detective Smalls said, struggling to maintain her already wavering patience.

Elizabeth tsked. "I don't know who killed her, but I hope you can figure it out because I want them put away behind bars. All I know is that the lights went out around midnight. There was a storm, so I just assumed the power had been knocked out, so I went to bed. There was nothing left to do in the dark…"

"And then?" Detective Smalls pushed.

"Then later, I woke up to noises… I came down the

steps, and she was just hanging there. Just like that. It was quite a shock. I'm still in shock, I think." For the first time, the detective could hear a quiver in the elderly woman's voice. "It was so awful… so sickening. I just don't know who would do such a thing."

"Perhaps it was the same person who wrote those mean, anonymous warnings to your daughter-in-law. Why did you write those things, Elizabeth? What could you possibly gain from ruining Rosalee's party, and life?" Detective Smalls leaned forward and placed her hands on the table. She spread her fingers.

Elizabeth's lips were pinched together, and her cheeks grew red. "Listen here. I never wrote anything mean to Rosalee. My anonymous note was something about not going to bed angry at night and to always tell your spouse that you love them no matter what. I lost my husband and the night before it happened, I'd gone to bed angry at him. And when he went back for surgery, I didn't even tell him I loved him or wished him goodbye…" The tough façade was fading now, Elizabeth's shoulders shaking with grief.

"I never tried to hurt Rosalee," she moaned. "Yes, I thought it was a bad idea, her and my son. I thought Georgia was more his type. But I was wrong about that … I've been wrong about so many things."

"I believe you. I don't think you wrote those notes," Detective Smalls said, softening her expression. Elizabeth

Beake was a tough cookie, but even the hardest cookies crumbled under pressure. There was more to this woman than met the eye. Behind the coldness and the harsh critiques was a sad, lonely woman. Detective Smalls hated that she recognized herself, albeit a much younger version, when she looked at Elizabeth Beake.

"There were text message exchanges between your daughter, Bri, and your son, Asher. They were angry at you. So angry that in one of those messages, your son said he could kill you for lying to him. What were they so angry about, Elizabeth?" the detective asked, switching gears.

Elizabeth released a deep sigh, slumping down in the chair.

"I didn't think they would find out, but of course they did. Nothing gets past that daughter of mine. She's still an emergency contact with release of information privileges on my medical records. I knew that, but I never expected that she was calling my primary care physician regularly, checking up on me and being nosy about my personal health," Elizabeth said.

"What did your daughter find out that you didn't want her to know?"

"My doctor told her about the cancer. So, of course she ran and told Asher too. They both want me to go through all the hoops and barrels—chemo and radiation. All that crap. But I told them, no way. And that's what I told my doctor too. I don't want to beat cancer. I'm ready to go and be with Edmund. If that makes my children angry, then so be it. It's not the first time I've been on somebody's bad side," Elizabeth said, with a huff.

"Tell me, Elizabeth. Who else's bad side were you on?"

"No one's. Everyone's! What do you want me to say here? I tend to rub people up the wrong way sometimes. I'm bold and outspoken. Sometimes I go too far…"

"Like when you purchased maternity garments as a gift for your son's fiancée?" the detective said, with a grimace. "I heard there was a confrontation about that earlier in the evening."

"Yes. Like that. I was wrong for doing that, okay? But my strained relationship with Rosalee and my recent diagnosis have nothing to do with what happened last night. I have no reason to hurt anyone."

"If not you, then who did? Who was that angry last night?"

"Everyone! We were all tense all weekend long, me included," Elizabeth said, with a sigh.

The detective stared at the woman, searching her face for clues. Elizabeth was adamant she had nothing to do with the murder. Perhaps *too* adamant and defensive…

"Out of everyone, whose behavior stood out the most to you yesterday? Was anyone behaving strangely?" the detective asked, carefully. Elizabeth didn't strike her as the kindest woman, but she was certainly observant.

"Well, if I had to pick one, I'd say Tinsley. She's a weird girl, so strange-looking and awkward... and I saw her creeping around the house a few times, doing things that didn't make sense to me."

"Doing things that didn't make sense ... like what, for example?" the detective leaned forward, closing the short space between them.

"It was like she was up to something in that house, always snooping around, like she thought nobody could see her. Yesterday, I was in the kitchen cleaning up and getting a drink, when she suddenly popped out of the pantry. It was the strangest damn thing. Nearly gave me a heart attack."

"The pantry?"

Elizabeth rolled her eyes. "You sure like to repeat yourself, officer. You remind me of my therapist," she said, with a gushing sigh. "Yes, the pantry," she said the words slowly, the words bitter on her tongue. "You know that place where people keep extra food and cleaning supplies?"

Now it was Detective Smalls' turn to roll her eyes. "Why did you consider that strange?"

"It wasn't strange that Tinsley went in the pantry, but the odd thing is... she was in there with the door closed and the lights turned out for a while, which took me by surprise when she emerged like a freakish ghoul. Something about that girl isn't right. I thought maybe she was hiding in there in the dark, waiting to spring out and attack someone. Maybe me…"

"Why would she want to do that, Elizabeth?"

Elizabeth huffed. "I have no idea. Maybe she was in there doing drugs. Who knows?"

The detective leaned back in her chair, scribbled something on the notebook in her lap, then ended the interview with Elizabeth Beake.

Chapter Twenty-Five

CRIME SCENE, WALKTHROUGH #2

Detective Nina Smalls' father was right about one thing—crime scenes are not the same when you return a second time. Or a third, or fourth…

But instead of seeing fewer details, this time, the detective sees more.

Alone in the mansion, she is able to appreciate the details this time around. The antique French furniture, the chandeliers and sconces, the high, old windows and strange art. The Leblanc-Landry mansion encompasses its history, although it's a darker story than some of the other nearby estates.

The detective was born in Louisiana, and she is familiar with most of the houses and properties in the city of New Orleans, some more than she would like to be. So, she is familiar with the tragic story of the Leblancs and the Landrys, and she knows that the property has changed hands many times over the last century. Currently, it belongs to a wealthy businessman, who owns nearly a dozen other rental properties in the city. He rents them out to tourists for exorbitant amounts; he doesn't even live in Louisiana, brokering out the upkeep and care of the properties to others. Many people in New Orleans despise opportunistic people like that.

The detective moves stealthily through the house, this time bypassing the dining area where the body was found.

She enters the library instead, a sudden draft sending chills up and down her back.

Her father talked a lot about intuition, and she believes strongly in that too. But more than imagination and intuition, she relies on science. Science tells the story better than her imagination ever could.

When she closes the door of the library and turns off the lights, photons come to life. They glow like a neon Pollock painting, telling a bloody tale.

The detective has already seen the photos, taken by crime scene technicians, an hour ago. But seeing them in person is different.

The book, used as a weapon, was obviously swung in an arc, striking the victim and creating the initial blow. But that wasn't enough, and the castoff on the wall behind the bookshelves shows that the killer swung the book back, striking a second time. *Was the second hit a fatal blow?* the detective wonders.

The blood on the floor tells another story. The victim hit the floor and tried to brace herself, bloody smears mark the books as she went down, and there's a smear on the floor as well.

The detective stares at the backside of the library door, turns her head sideways as she studies the castoff on the wall.

If the victim died here, then she would have been carried or dragged from this room. But there are no smears of blood on the carpet near the library door, no gruesome trails showing where the body was slid across the marble...

The luminol tells a gruesome story, but there's still part of it missing.

How did one killer lift the victim out of this room, leaving no blood trail, and then lift her overhead, slip the noose over her neck, and send her into the rafters... without any help?

Minutes pass, maybe hours, as the detective studies the blood in the library. Was it possible the victim was struck twice in this room, but didn't die? She got up from the floor, nursing a head wound, and walked out of here on her own...?

Finally, the detective heads for the kitchen, entering through the swinging doors.

It's an industrial-sized kitchen, not like anything you'd see in a normal house. Certainly built for staff and servants at the turn of the century, not a modern-day family.

There are two rooms connected to the backside of the kitchen, a large washroom for staff, and a utility room with two sets of modern washers and dryers for laundry. Next to these, the detective locates the breaker box.

Back when the house was originally built, there was no electricity just candlelight and kerosene. But the breaker had been installed at some point and then updated with a modern set-up, probably by the current owner.

The panel had already been dusted for prints earlier, smudges smear the front door and inside of the box itself.

Carefully, the detective flips each switch, casting the house in darkness. Just like it was last night.

The detective uses her phone light as a torch, making her way back to the kitchen from the breaker box. Moonlight seeps in through the old windows; tendrils of light climb the ceiling and walls, casting eerie shadows in the dark. The detective's heart rate quickens. She tries to channel her father's steely reserve.

She moves to the pantry door, takes the bronze knob in her hand, and turns it.

Inside, the pantry is just like Elizabeth Beake

described. Shelves lined with canned goods and boxed food, extra paper and household supplies. But the detective isn't interested in the pantry's contents, she's interested in the butler's quarters.

After talking to Elizabeth about the pantry and Tinsley's odd behavior, she pulls up blueprints of the mansion online. She can easily see the small garret rooms that were essentially 'invisible' to most people in the nineteenth century. Back then, and still sometimes today, servants were kept out of sight and out of mind, as they were more a part of the house and woodwork itself instead of real people working for the family. The butler's pantry was part of this.

In reality, the entrance isn't hidden at all. Not if you're looking for it.

The back wall of the pantry is mostly empty and cleared of goods in one section of the wall, and the knob to the butler's door is clearly visible when the detective shines her torch upon it.

The detective turns the knob and nudges inward on the shelf with her shoulder; the entrance to the butler's quarters opens easily before her like a wide, gaping mouth. She thinks about the protagonists in horror movies, always merging straight ahead into darkness, going against human nature and natural instinct.

But cops are taught to do this every day. Run toward

the gunman, step into the shootout, put yourself in harm's way...

She steps into the dark opening in the pantry and shines her light around.

A tightly wound staircase ascends above her, revealing her theory was right. Tinsley had probably discovered, or already knew about, this secret servants' wing of the house.

The detective climbs the twisty stairs, holding her light up with one hand, swatting at a few loose cobwebs with the other. She's not afraid of many things, but she detests small creatures with many legs. Spiders are the worst, followed closely by those alien-like centipedes.

At the very top of the staircase, she shivers, wishing she had turned the breaker back on before venturing into this unknown, and possibly unsafe, part of the house. Who knew how long it had been since these quarters were used?

The detective has a bad habit of playing out every scenario in times of danger, her mind drifting to the darkest places. She imagines what would happen if the stairs collapsed and she fell, if not to her death than to a fate of broken bones in the very least. How long would it be until her assistant or one of the technicians returned and found her?

She pushes herself forward, hyper-focused on the task in hand.

The top landing opens into a single room, but it is a large one, housing several sinks and rows of cabinetry; in one corner, there is an antique wardrobe and wrought-iron bed. This was definitely where the head butler or maid slept back in the day, she realized.

The cabinets reveal very little—mothballs and mouse turds, a couple of old cans of paint and cleaners. But the wardrobe tells a different story.

Inside, the detective finds modern clothing. Plain blouses on wire hangers and neatly folded stacks of pants. Someone has been hiding in the servants' quarters…

Below the stack of neat pants, she finds a box—inside is a wet and dirty pair of pants and a shirt that appears to be stained with blood.

Chapter Twenty-Six

INTERVIEW: SUSPECT #3

"Let me get straight to the point. Why did you hide bloody clothes in the butler's chambers? You had to know we would eventually find them, and your DNA is probably all over them. It's only a matter of a time before we know the truth…" the detective warned.

Tinsley was shaking, her shoulders and hands quivering uncontrollably behind the interrogation table. But when the detective asked that question, about the butler's chamber, her demeanor completely changed.

Tinsley slammed her fists down on the table, giving the detective a jolt.

"Fuck you, lady!" she shouted. "I didn't hide anything, and I didn't kill her. I don't even step on spiders when I see them. And let me tell you, I really fucking hate bugs." Tinsley dropped her shoulders back and puffed out her chest. But the anger and momentum she'd felt drizzled out moments later when the detective remained still, watching her suspect shiver with anxiety and fear.

"Why were you in the pantry, Tinsley? I know you found the butler's quarters…"

"Of course I knew! I was interested in the house, okay? I like old houses and ghostly shit. So, I went exploring a bit on Saturday and I found the entrance to the butler's pantry. I'd read about it online. It's not that big of a secret for people who actually read and like to research things."

"A convenient excuse. That way when we find your prints and DNA all over that butler's room, you'll have an excuse for being in there. Simply exploring…" The detective throws up her hands. She's short on sleep and even shorter on patience.

"No, actually, you won't find much of anything belonging to me in there," Tinsley said. "I opened the door, but I never made it up the steps. I heard someone come in the kitchen. That damn Beake woman. I thought about going up there anyway, but then I decided against it. I was going to come back later and explore, but I never got the chance. I closed the door to the butler's chamber, and I never went back to it. The only place you'll find my prints is on the knob and doorway."

The detective frowned, considering the girl's open

and honest expression. The closer she got to the truth, the farther she felt from understanding anything.

Shifting gears, she asked, "What did you write on Rosalee's anonymous well wish card? Do you remember?"

Tinsley shrunk back into her chair and started picking at her fingers nervously.

"I don't remember, exactly."

"You don't remember? Well, surely you can recall the gist of it, at least…"

"I don't know, okay? It was something about not going to bed angry. Something dumb and cheesy, like a quote from a Hallmark card."

"That's not true though, is it?"

Tinsley looked up into the detective's eyes, deer in headlights. "What do you mean?"

"Elizabeth Beake wrote the one about going to bed angry. You just heard that one read aloud by Rosalee so you claimed it was yours before she could call you out on the real thing you wrote."

Tinsley placed her face in her hands.

The detective waited; patience restored.

Finally, with a voice resembling that of a tiny bird, Tinsley said quietly, "I only did it because I felt like she needed to be honest. Honesty is everything, you know? How was she going to marry that man and join his family, how could she call those people her friends… if they didn't know the truth about what she did?"

"What she did?"

Tinsley frowned.

"Maybe I should get a lawyer," she said suddenly, sticking out her chin.

The detective shrugged, leaning back in her chair. She said nothing.

But Tinsley was stubborn too, letting the minutes pass by slowly, and quietly.

"You think the truth should be out in the open. That's why you wrote the note about Rosalee's secrets… well, come on then, Tinsley. Let's hear it. Tell me what Rosalee did that was so bad."

Tinsley closed her eyes and took a deep breath. "Rosalee killed her father."

Chapter Twenty-Seven

INTERVIEW: SUSPECT #4

"Where were you when the lights went out last night?" the detective asked.

Bri Beake, like so many of the other women from the party, was shaken and distraught. But her shakiness seemed less like nervousness, and more like the telltale signs of someone who needed a stiff drink or a hit from their favorite drug. Detective Nina Smalls should know —her father had suffered from alcohol addiction throughout most of his career. That's why she refused to touch the stuff now.

"I was upstairs in my room, trying to sleep. I'd had too much to drink. We all had. And things were tense when we got back to the house from Bourbon Street. Mara seemed determined to get everyone riled up and we all went our separate ways after the gathering at the firepit," Bri said.

Detective Smalls said nothing.

"Do you know who did this?"

"Not yet," the detective answered, honestly.

"Well, why are you wasting your time on me, then? I certainly didn't do it. What reason would I have for killing her?"

"You tell me." The detective shrugged.

Bri groaned. "We've been here for nearly twenty-four hours now, it seems! This isn't right. We are in shock, and we're traumatized... and we've already missed our flight home! If you don't release me soon, I'm going to call my brother. He's a lawyer. Did you know that?"

The detective clicked her pen, open and closed.

Finally, she said, "No one is accusing you of anything, Bri. I'm just trying to get to the bottom of things. When the lights went out, you stayed in bed. Correct?"

Bri drummed her fingers on the desk, impatiently. "Yes, I told the other detectives that when they wrote down my initial statement."

"The lights went out a little after midnight. But you didn't find the body until almost 3:30 a.m."

"Yes. For the millionth time," Bri cried in exasperation.

"The electricity had been restored by the time you came downstairs. You walked down the steps, turned into the dining room, and that's when you saw the body hanging from the rafters?"

"Yes," Bri said.

"There were storms earlier that day, but there were no reported power outages in the area. Someone must have flipped the breakers."

Bri's mouth fell open in surprise. "I didn't realize that," she said, sounding humble for the first time all night.

"What woke you at three in the morning? That's one thing you haven't explained," the detective said, glancing down at her notebook. The pages were mostly blank, the book itself more for show than anything.

I keep it all up here, her father used to say, tapping a pen on the side of his head.

"Honestly, I'm not sure. I've never been a very good sleeper. Most nights at home, I suffer from insomnia. I'd had too much to drink, like I said earlier, so I got up and went downstairs for some water."

"And you saw no one else in the hallway or downstairs?"

Bri shook her head.

"And you're sure nothing in particular woke you? No sounds?"

Bri shook her head again. "Not that I'm aware of."

Internally, the detective was screaming. She felt like she was getting nowhere, circling around a drain.

"Would you like something to drink right now, Bri? You do look really thirsty."

Bri groaned.

"I drink too much alcohol, okay? And I got drunk a lot this weekend. I also abuse my anti-anxiety meds. But that doesn't mean I hurt anyone."

Detective Smalls held up her hands. "I agree with that, Bri. My father had an alcohol problem too. That's not what I'm implying here."

Bri chewed her lip. "I do remember seeing Tinsley right before I went to bed. Her room was next to mine, and we gave each other a look before we went into our rooms. I think we were all just ready to go home. The party started out disastrously and ended in much the same way."

"Obviously, it was a disaster. That's putting it mildly. Someone has been murdered," the detective said, narrowing her eyes. Bri reminded the detective of her mother, Elizabeth. Cold and calculated, at times, focused only on how things affected her.

"I know that someone was murdered, okay? And I feel fucking terrible about it! I'm just saying that shit was bad before whoever killed her struck," Bri explained.

The detective needed to switch gears again, reestablish some sort of rapport with her suspect. Lack of sleep and frustration weren't getting her anywhere...

"Your mother said you were upset because of her

cancer diagnosis. I can imagine you were pretty stressed out about that this weekend. She said you had just found out, you and your brother."

Bri sighed. "Yeah, you can say that again. My mom, the toughest person I've ever met, won't even attempt to fight this stupid disease. It pisses me off. And it pissed off my brother too. She should have told us sooner. But that has nothing to do with what happened tonight."

"I looked into your company. It's a start-up, right?" the detective said, looking at her blank papers again.

"Yeah. We build computers and help businesses launch websites…"

It hasn't been as profitable as you probably would have hoped for so far," the detective said.

"Again, what does that have to do with anything?" Bri said, exasperated.

"Did you ask your mother for money? For help?"

Bri shook her head. "Of course not. My mom has enough to worry about."

"What about your brother or his fiancé?"

"Nope. Not them either. I was figuring it out on my own," Bri said, crossing her arms over her chest.

"You know, they say that more money gets stolen with a pen than a sword," Detective Smalls said, lifting her own ink pen in the air.

"Okay…"

"I know about the investor who screwed you out of

tens of thousands of dollars. Not a lot in your mother's eyes, but for you... that was probably devastating," the detective said, solemnly.

"Yeah, well... shit happens."

"Does it?" the detective asked. "Because that seems pretty unusual."

Bri wrung her hands together, throat dry and scratchy. "Who told you about that?"

"Your employees. When I talked to them on the phone, they were more than willing to share this information. I think they thought I was calling to help. But you never reported the incident to the police. Why not?"

Bri shrugged. "It's embarrassing, okay? I was so excited to get an investor and they seemed legit. I didn't realize that I was transferring money to a god damn hacker."

"You must have been angry. Did you ever find out who was behind it? You're pretty savvy with computers, you graduated from the best computer college on the planet. Surely, you tried to figure out this hacker situation on your own," the detective said.

Bri frowned. "I wish it were that easy, detective, but it's not. The email and IP address were untraceable. If I can't track them down, then the cops can't either. It was a huge loss. But I tightened up my ship and let it go."

"But filing a police report on the incident wouldn't have hurt," the detective said.

"That's where you're wrong. Try selling yourself as a computer guru to software companies when you can't even prevent your own self from being hacked. That would be stupid to share publicly, catch my drift?" Bri said.

"I suppose," the detective said. "I want to ask you one more thing, Bri. Did you write the anonymous note to Rosalee, telling her to make sure she sexually satisfies her husband, so you don't have to?"

Bri's mouth fell open in surprise, and then she tilted her head back and laughed. "No, of course not. Why the hell would I say that about my own brother?"

"To make it seem like your brother had a side piece. To stir up drama, perhaps?"

"I wouldn't do that. I'm many things, and some of those things aren't good. But I am loyal to my brother. I'd never tell a lie about him," Bri said.

"Then who would?" the detective pressed.

"I know who wrote it, but it wasn't true. My brother only had eyes for Rosalee," Bri said, with a tight, knowing smile.

"Who wrote it then, Bri?"

She leaned back in her chair and dropped her hands on the table. "It was Mara, okay? She admitted it to me while she was drunk our first night at the house. She thought my brother really might be sleeping with Georgia, and she wanted Rosalee to confront her about it. But I told her that was ridiculous, my brother and Georgia have always just been friends. I think she felt bad for writing it, but by then, it was too late to tell Rosalee the truth without making her hate her for it..."

The detective nodded and pushed back her chair. "That's all for now. Thanks, Bri."

"Can I get that drink now? Maybe a coke? I bet you have some Scotch in your drawer somewhere."

Chapter Twenty-Eight

INTERVIEW: SUSPECT #5

"Out of everyone at the party, you had the most reason to feel angry and betrayed," the detective said, bracing herself against the table, unable to sit anymore. After more than twenty-four hours without sleep, and her body surging with adrenaline, she felt strangely keyed up and exhausted all at once, her eyelids leaden and her ass numb from sitting in the interview chair. She was itching to return to the crime scene—the scene itself seemed to provide more helpful information than this cluster of troubled women...

Rosalee Mumford stared the detective straight in the face, unflinching. But she didn't answer the question. In fact, she hadn't said a single word since telling the police she wanted to wait for her lawyer husband.

Her friends had described her as nice—too nice, at

times—but she wasn't giving off soft, flowery vibes tonight. Not to the detective, at least.

According to Detective Smalls' deputies, Rosalee's husband was on his way. His plane was scheduled to land in just a few hours. He was an attorney and Rosalee wanted him there beside her. It was only by the grace of god that he hadn't shown up already, his original flight cancelled and then postponed again due to weather. *The longer I can keep the lawyer away, the better*, the detective thought, wearily.

Her silence made sense, certainly. She was soon-to-be-married to a lawyer. Normal, everyday people want to talk: the guilty, so they can weasel their way out of trouble, and the innocent, to tell their side of things and prove they aren't capable of whatever crime they're suspected of committing.

But people who have been through the system often, and those familiar with law enforcement and the judicial system—they often know better. They rarely waive their right to an attorney.

She might be too nice, but she certainly isn't gullible, the detective thought, studying the young, stoic woman sitting at the table across from her. From what the detective could gather from the other women, and sources close to her, Rosalee was smart and kind, creative… and also damaged.

She had lost her parents at a very young age.

Tragedies like those are hard to overcome; one minute you think you're unaffected by the past, and the next minute, the ripples of what you've been through are creating waves and eventual tsunamis in every avenue of your life.

Detective Smalls should know—she, too, lost her mother tragically at an early age. Suicide. Peyton Smalls, who suffered with untreated depression her whole life, had finally given into her demons and leapt from a bridge, falling a hundred feet to her death. Just to make sure she finished the job, she chose the only bridge in the city with no water below.

Luckily for the detective, she was younger than Rosalee when it happened. She didn't know or understand what had happened to her mother, only that she had gone to heaven according to her father and other family. Not until many years later did she learn the truth about her mother's death.

"Look, I understand if you don't want to talk. To be honest, I probably wouldn't talk either if I were in your situation. Asher will be here soon, so hopefully you'll be ready to talk then."

Silence.

"But I do want you to know that you're the only one who hasn't spoken to me so far. Everyone else has given their side of the story and told me what they know…"

Detective Smalls pulled out her chair and forced

herself to stop pacing and take a seat across from Rosalee. They stared each other down for what felt like minutes, and then the detective started talking.

"I don't need you to talk. I just want you to listen. Okay?"

Rosalee's head tilted slightly to the side, and the detective assumed that meant yes.

"Everyone had a reason to be mad at someone at that party. The lights went out suspiciously and now I'm wondering… perhaps she wasn't even the intended victim. Perhaps one of you was going after someone else and got her by mistake in the dark…"

Rosalee closed her eyes, lip trembling. It was the first real sign of emotion from her that the detective had seen.

The detective continued, hoping she could break her down enough to talk before the lawyer husband swooped in and closed the whole thing down.

"But you … you had a reason to hate them all. Didn't you?"

Rosalee opened her eyes and creased her brows, apparently in confusion.

"Your mother-in-law was awful to you. She didn't like you very much, did she? And your sister-in-law was much the same. They seem like two birds of a feather, as the saying goes…

"And don't get me started on Georgia Britt. I'm not married myself, but I can only imagine how it feels to have your boyfriend hanging around with a girl who looks like Georgia all the time. Their whole friendship seems a little strange, right? And Tinsley. We have to talk about Tinsley, don't we, Rosalee?"

Rosalee didn't react as she stared down at her hands; palms pressed firmly on the table, fingers spread, skin turning white from the pressure. *What is she hiding from me?* the detective wondered. She fought the urge to reach out and shake the woman. *Tell me what you know!* She wanted to shout.

Detective Smalls was tired, running solely on caffeine and adrenaline. If her father were here, he would have had the sense to take a break or let one of the deputies step in and take over the interviews for a while.

But unlike her father, Detective Smalls had a compulsion—when she started working on a case, especially a homicide like this one, she couldn't think about a single thing until it was solved. A blessing and a curse, when you work in a field that solves far fewer murders than they'd lead one to believe on TV crime dramas...

"Tinsley and you were very close. She said that you moved in with her after your parents' accident. She described you as a sister. It's funny how someone could say that, on the one hand, but on the other... she could write those terrible words."

Rosalee's eyes shifted from the table to the detective's, curiosity getting the better of her.

"We found the anonymous well wishes your friends gave you. A couple of them weren't very sweet, especially the one about knowing all your secrets and how your husband would soon know them too."

If the detective expected a reaction out of Rosalee when she said this, she didn't get one. In fact, Rosalee was picking at her cuticles now, looking bored.

"Tinsley admitted that she wrote that one," the detective said.

Rosalee lifted her eyes in what seemed to be genuine surprise.

"I also know who wrote the other one, about satisfying Asher so she no longer has to do it for you," the detective said, boldly.

"Who?" Rosalee spoke for the first time, surprising the detective and herself.

The detective tried not to overreact to the sound of the woman's voice, but she couldn't hold back a small, triumphant smile. She lifted one finger. "We'll get to that. But first, I want to finish talking about Tinsley. What secret did she know about you, Rosalee? What was she threatening to tell everyone?"

Rosalee shook her head back and forth. "Like I said earlier, I'm not talking until my fiancé gets here. He can answer your questions then."

"Fair enough. But, if I'm being honest here, then I must admit that I already know the answer. Tinsley believes you killed your father. That's the secret she's been holding for you."

Rosalee stared at her hands, but her shoulders lifted, tightening up around her ears.

"I pulled up everything I could find on your parents' accident. It was an awful snowstorm, a total whiteout. No one was supposed to be on the road. But you and your parents were out that day for some reason. Your father was driving, and your mother was in the passenger's seat. And you Rosalee... you were riding in the back, weren't you?"

Silence.

"What happened was awful and I don't want to make you relive that, I really don't. I, too, lost a parent at an early age. Things like that... well, they fuck you up. I should know."

Rosalee cleared her throat. "Sorry for your loss," she said, croakily, but then said nothing more.

"Your mother died on impact according to the report. Your father wasn't wearing a seatbelt when he hit that tree and he was flung through the windshield. He died not too long after, succumbing to blood loss and the harsh winter elements. And you... you were left there alone, for nearly a day and a half, before someone found you. I can't imagine how horrible that must have been for you. How scary. I can't imagine what something like that does to a person…"

"I can tell you what it doesn't do. It doesn't make them a murderer, if that's what you're implying," Rosalee said, writhing in her seat.

I need to find a way to keep her talking, the detective thought, desperate for answers.

"It certainly doesn't. You're right. So, why does your cousin believe that you killed your father? Or, let me put it this way: why did you tell her that you killed him, Rosalee?"

Rosalee's tough mask slipped, eyes crinkling in the corners and voice quivering as she said, "Because I wish I had."

"How come?"

Rosalee shook her head, but she couldn't stop the tears. They bubbled over, running down her cheeks. She tried to wipe them with the back of her hands, but now they were coming too fast.

"It's okay. I just want to know why. I'm not accusing you of doing anything to anyone. I'm just trying to understand what Tinsley's mindset was, why she would say such terrible things about you."

"It's not her fault, it's mine. She's right—I told her that I killed him, okay? And even now, I still wish it were true. I wanted to be the one who killed him. I wanted to put that mean old man out of his misery for good," Rosalee said.

"What did he do to you, Rosalee? Please tell me," the detective said, softly.

"Nothing. He was kind to me, if anything. That's what always made it so hard. It was my mother he mistreated, beating her and tormenting her every chance he had, and then morphing back into this charming and wonderful guy she thought she could trust. He was mad at her that day. He was always mad about something ... and the drive was his way of punishing her. She had been talking on the phone to one of her male coworkers. So, of course he accused her of cheating. He forced us out into the car, even though no one was supposed to be on the roads that day because of the weather. It wasn't the first time he used his vehicle as a weapon, driving recklessly or swerving to spook my mom when he was angry. Riding with him was always terrifying, no matter what sort of mood he was in. And regardless of the road or weather conditions."

"Did he crash the car on purpose that day?"

Rosalee took a sharp intake of breath, then sighed heavily. "I don't know, truly. I don't think so. I think he simply didn't see the tree ahead. He was screaming at my mom, holding the wheel with one hand and punching her with his fist in the other. I kept putting my head down in my lap, praying and waiting. The best way to deal with his angry outbursts was just to ride them out. Eventually, he would exhaust himself and run out of steam, just like a toddler throwing a tantrum. But then the crash happened. And when I came to, my mother was dead and my father was gone, a big, jagged hole in the windshield showing me where he went."

"How long did he live, Rosalee?"

"I don't know, exactly. An hour or two. I was hurt, a few broken ribs and a cracked collarbone, I'd later find out… but I climbed out and went to him. I tried to help him. But he was too heavy, and he was bleeding so much…"

"You were lucky you lived that day," the detective said.

Rosalee didn't respond.

"I'm so sorry you went through that, but why does Tinsley think you had something to do with it?"

Rosalee frowned. "Because I lied to her. I lied to the police then, too. I told everyone who would listen that he killed my mother and that after he crashed and killed her, I picked up a big boulder and smashed it down over his head."

"Why? Why would you tell them that?"

"Because that's what I wish I had done. But instead, I lay on the ground and cried for him. And I hated myself even more… for loving my father even after I knew what he was. An abuser, a killer, an awful person…" Rosalee sobbed.

"Oh, Rosalee. I'm sorry."

Rosalee waved off the detective's apology. "I'm over it now," she sniffed, trying to put a brave mask on. "Truly, I am. But, somehow, telling that story back then made me feel better after it happened. I channeled all of the grief and pain over the loss of my mother... I channeled it into rage. I told that story about killing him so many times over the years to Tinsley, that I truly think I started to believe it myself after a while. Even now, it's hard to reconcile reality with the fiction I spun in its aftermath."

The detective understood this, in her own way. There were so many times when she lied and created her own stories about her mother growing up. *Mom is a super model who travels the world and that's why she can't be with me.* Or, *mom was a modern-day Evil Knievel, trying to achieve a new base-jumping record when her parachute failed, and the stunt went horribly wrong and that's how she fell...*

And then there were times when the detective softened the story, telling her childhood friends that her mother died of cancer or from a heart attack. People seemed to feel sorrier for those who died of a disease that wasn't invisible like depression.

"You never told Tinsley the truth?" the detective asked, finally, swallowing the lump in her throat.

"No. Because like I said, I wanted to believe it too.

And telling her my secret brought us closer together, even if that secret was a big fat lie. The police and emergency workers who rescued me knew the truth... It was clear that my dad died of his injuries and the cold, and I wasn't strong enough to lift a boulder like that over him anyway. I think they felt sorry for me for the lies. They just nodded and went along with it, then shipped me off to live with my aunt and cousin. The rest is history."

"Thank you for explaining that to me," the detective said, sincerely. "I think you need to also explain it to Tinsley soon, when you get a chance. Because she believes it, wholeheartedly, and that's why she wrote that note. I think she truly believes you're hiding the truth of your past from your future family."

Rosalee nodded.

"I suppose, in a way, you are. They deserve to know what you've gone through. Perhaps they would be kinder to you if they knew the truth. Did your friend Mara think you killed your father too?" the detective asked, tentatively.

Rosalee's head drooped.

"Come on, Rosalee. You've already talked to me about Tinsley. I think it's finally time for us to discuss Mara, too."

Rosalee's eyes were flooding with tears again, her body shaking with grief.

"We've examined all of Mara's belongings that were in her room. I found a notebook in her bag where she was practicing writing her well wishes to you, too."

Rosalee used her sleeve to wipe a drizzle of snot from her nostrils. "Okay, so?"

"So, she's the one who wrote the note about sexually satisfying your future husband."

Rosalee froze.

"She admitted to Bri when she was drunk that she wrote it. I don't think she was actually sleeping with him. She just wanted to rile you up and get you to confront Georgia..." the detective revealed.

Rosalee was shaking her head from side to side, as though she wanted to loosen the spinning thoughts in her head.

"Tell me, Rosalee. Is that the reason you killed your best friend?"

Chapter Twenty-Nine

INTERVIEW: SUSPECT #6

"How long have you worked at the Leblanc-Landry mansion?"

Delfina shifted nervously in her chair. She was wearing a stiff white uniform, as though she were still serving food for guests. But her eyes were red-rimmed and puffy, as though she'd been crying.

"I don't know. Eleven or twelve years, maybe?" she said, timidly.

The detective nodded, scribbling down the answer in her notebook. She then continued to click the retractable pen open and closed several times, then she set it back down on the table.

"Delfina, how many parties have you hosted there?"

Delfina looked startled by the question. "I don't

know. I don't keep track, ma'am. Probably a thousand, or more."

"A thousand. Wow, that's a lot. And do you always stay on the property during these events?" the detective asked.

Delfina picked at a loose string on her blouse, refusing to meet the detective's eye. "Sometimes. It depends on what is asked of me," she said, in a faint voice.

"And what was asked of you this time, for this particular party?"

"To manage the food and cleanup on the day of their arrival and then to serve appetizers on Saturday. They mostly wanted help with the food. We came a few hours before to prep, me and my six-person staff team. We were all there during dinner too, then we cleaned up and left. I returned alone on Saturday and brought their hors d'oeuvres, but they weren't back yet since they were out on the town."

"So, they didn't ask you to stay on the property then. Correct?" the detective pressed.

Delfina was silent.

"Delfina…"

"No, they did not," she said, finally, eyes flickering up to the detective's, but only for a brief moment.

"Then why were you there all weekend? I found some of your things in the butler's pantry room. You were there all along, you never left. Your staff went home, but you never did… Why?"

Delfina shrugged. "I thought that I might be needed. Especially after what happened with the girl on Friday. I was worried about her! She had an allergic reaction and I felt responsible."

"But that wasn't your fault, Delfina. Mara orchestrated that on purpose."

Delfina narrowed her eyes, then opened her mouth and quickly closed it.

"There are a lot of clothes in the pantry room, Delfina. I think you might be staying there all the time. I'm sure you don't make a lot of money working at the house. and the owner lives out of state, so would never find out. I can see why you might just stay in those hidden quarters… I would be tempted to do that myself."

"It's just easier this way. I clean the house and get it ready for the next guests. And I always stay out of their way. I don't make a nuisance of myself. And I know that house better than anyone," Delfina said, sitting up straighter in her chair.

"There's only one problem though. I found blood and dirt on some of the clothes, Delfina. Something happened. Maybe Mara said something to you? Pissed you off somehow? I know you tried to hide the clothes afterwards, but what I don't understand is why. She was pissing everyone off all weekend. What did she do to set you off?"

Delfina's eyes were round as quarters. "I didn't kill anyone, ma'am. I swear I didn't."

"But those were your stained clothes I found, right?"

Delfina's face crumbled.

The detective watched and waited, as the woman lowered her head and sobbed.

"It's okay. You can tell me what happened. We're just talking here," the detective said, reaching out to pat the woman's hand.

Delfina pulled back. "I didn't kill anybody. You must believe me! I just helped with the mess. I didn't want to lose my job or cost the other workers their jobs either! I knew that if people thought she was murdered on the property, it would come with lawsuits and lengthy investigations. The guests were rich, okay? And the bride's future husband is a bigshot lawyer. But suicide… that seemed like a better option. I didn't hurt anyone, I just put her up there with the rope so it would look like it was her own doing. We depend on these jobs… This is all we have… Please…"

Chapter Thirty

CRIME SCENE, WALKTHROUGH #3

"Have you ever heard that expression: 'Silence is deafening'?" Officer Smalls' assistant asks her.

Here they are, back in the carriageway of the Leblanc-Landry mansion, the assistant's second visit and the detective's third in just under thirty-six hours.

The assistant's eyes are droopy. His limbs are heavy. He feels punch-drunk without the punch.

"Yes, I've heard it," the detective says, pressing her gloved hand to the exterior door. It opens with barely more than a nudge, creaking eerily in the night-time silence.

There is no one on the other side of it.

"That's just creepy as hell," the assistant mutters, pointing at the door. "Like some phantom butler letting people in and out any time they touch the door…"

The detective stops in the open doorway, listening. You could have heard a pin drop—her assistant is right, the silence here is loud. Not even the ticking of clocks or the buzz of night-time critters outside.

She shuts the door behind the two of them.

"It's not really all that creepy, Matthias. On the surface, yes, but most strange incidents have a perfectly logical explanation. For example…"

The detective squats down behind the door, shining her heavy Maglite at the hinges while Matthias recovers from the shock of realizing she actually knows his name.

Detective Smalls stands up, reaches in her back pocket, and removes a small set of tools.

"Screws on the hinge need tightening, that's all. This little screwdriver is junk, but it's all I've got."

He watches her, mesmerized as she tightens the screws. He never carries tools on him, but he will after tonight.

Detective Smalls opens and closes the door several times, pleased with her work. The door won't creak open again on its own, at least not for a while.

"Now. Let's get on with the real mystery. Who killed our girl?" she says, raising a brow at Matthias. He likes her more by the day… by the second…

"Follow me," Detective Smalls says, and Matthias falls into step beside her.

She leads him back down the long dark hallway, and to the dining hall once more.

"Bri Beake found Mara Mattingly hanging dead from the rafters at approximately 3:30 a.m. She screamed, alerting the others. Within minutes, all five women were in the dining room, staring at their so-called friend's dead body. It was Rosalee herself who dialed 911 and alerted the authorities," the detective states, matter-of-factly.

The body is gone now, tucked away on ice at the local morgue, and soon to receive a full-scale autopsy that will hopefully tell them anything that they have missed.

The food still rots on the table. It smells like carnage and death, a sharp piercing smell that makes Matthias' belly twist and claws at the back of his throat. The odor seems to have no effect on his mentor, or else, she hides it well.

"Someone killed her and then the maid hung her corpse up to make it look like a suicide…," Matthias says, breathlessly, staring at the phantom body he can still see in his mind. It swings there, eerie yet calm, those cold dead eyes staring back at him.

He will probably never erase that image of Mara Mattingly, no matter how hard he tries. It is burned onto his retinas, etched in the grooves of his cerebral cortex.

"Or it's possible that the maid and her staff both killed and strung her up. We don't know that she is telling the truth, Detective Smalls says. She whips around, leading her assistant room by room, eventually stopping at the library again. This room, with all its knowledge, puzzles her more than any other.

"This still bothers me," she says, nodding at the blood pool illuminated by luminol on the floor, and the spatter on the ceiling behind it.

"Yeah, it's super disturbing," Matthias says, then shudders.

"Look beyond that, Matthias. Yeah, it's a lot of blood, but where is the rest of it? If the killer dragged the body out of here and into the dining room, where is the blood trail? There should be a bloody streak from here, all the way to the dining room. Delfina said that she found the body right here in the dining room, but it can't be the truth. There's no trail…"

"Maybe the killer cleaned it up so well that we can't see the trail with the luminol. I mean, it is possible. I've read cases…"

The detective tilts her head from side to side, still trying to see it. "It is possible, you're right about that. But tell me—if they went to all that trouble cleaning up their trail, then why skip cleaning in here? Makes no sense."

"Perhaps someone walked in and caught them before they could finish cleaning? Perhaps they were interrupted?" Matthias says, voice quickening with excitement.

The detective held up a finger, as though listening for something. "Maybe. It's possible. But the lights weren't out for that long. A couple hours, tops. How could they kill a person and string them up in such little time? Something is missing here," she murmurs.

The phone in Matthias's pocket vibrates to life causing them both to jump with surprise.

"Yes?" he says, lifting the phone to his ear. His eyes are trained on Detective Smalls, who slowly inspects the books again. One is still missing, bagged up as evidence back at the station.

"Excuse me. What did you just say?" Matthias says to the caller, plugging a finger in his other ear. He heard the words correctly the first time.

"I think you'd better tell that to my boss." He passes the phone to the senior detective.

"This is Nina Smalls," she says, in her curt voice, still examining the heavy tomes on the shelves.

"Wait. What?" Detective Smalls spins on her heels, eyes widening at her assistant. "You've got to be kidding me," she says. Matthias watches her, as she silently listens to the medical examiner's findings on the other end of the line. It is too soon for the full autopsy results, but she already has a pretty clear idea of the cause of death.

When Detective Smalls hangs up the phone, she hands it back to Matthias.

"I guess our adventure extends to the pool, then. Now that we know our victim died by drowning," she says, with a heavy sigh.

In the pale moonlight, the pool water looks dark and inky, like a hideous black portal to another world. It has a mineral smell to it, eggy and clean, but noxious all the same.

The detective walks the perimeter of the pool, getting down on her knees and back up again several times as she studies the water's edge.

As she reaches the side of the pool nearest to the house, she freezes at one section of concrete. Down she goes, back on her knees, only this time, she holds her face, pressed to the ground, for several long minutes.

Matthias is getting antsy, uncomfortable with the silence.

Finally, the detective stands, glancing up at the second-story windows above.

"Stay here," she tells Matthias, then takes off at a jog back inside the house.

Alone by the poolside, Matthias is becoming cold. The wind shifts through the trees, a sticky breeze blowing the leaves and making the hair on his arms stand on end.

"Up here!" Detective Smalls calls, her voice singsongy in the dark. Mattias looks up from the spot she told him to stand by and sees her there, peering over the balcony at him. The bedroom doors behind her are flung open, billowy white curtains blowing in the wind.

He watches, in horror, as the detective lifts herself up on the railing, testing its strength.

"Be careful," he warns, voice barely above a whisper.

The detective leans her body, balancing on the edge, looking directly down at him... or rather, past him, to the concrete siding of the pool. It is only now that he sees it —a small, jagged chunk missing from the edge.

"We need the technicians back out here," the detective shouts in the wind. "I think Mara jumped or fell. Possibly she was pushed... and she hit her head before tumbling into the pool..."

By the time the detective runs back down the stairs, Matthias is on the phone with the main crime scene tech. He's also digging through the heavy shrubbery around the pool, looking for things they might have missed.

"Detective..."

Carefully, he uses a gloved hand to lift a plastic bag that was stuffed inside the branchy middle of the bush. Carefully, he peeks inside it.

A pillowcase is stuffed inside, and a heavy splotch of blood stains the center of it.

Chapter Thirty-One

INTERVIEW 2: SUSPECT #3

"I was wrong about the bloody clothes in the butler's pantry. They belonged to Delfina. She and one of her crew—she hasn't told us which one yet, but she will eventually—hung the body from the rafters. They got wet and bloody in the process. Sorry for accusing you."

Tinsley crossed her arms over her chest. "I told you I didn't kill her. So, it was the workers who did it? But why? What reason could they possibly have for killing Mara? It's not like they knew her."

The detective smiled, lips stretching slow and wide. "I didn't say they killed her."

"Okay…"

"Like I said, I was wrong about the wet, bloody clothes in the maid's quarters. But I wasn't wrong, not completely. You did hide something, Tinsley. All I need to know now is why."

Tinsley groaned. "I don't know what you're talking about…"

"Each room came equipped with two standard white pillowcases and two decorative shams, as well as two sets of sheets and a fitted comforter. So it wasn't hard to figure out which room was missing a pillowcase. You're the only guest without two in your room…"

"Well, I guess they can just charge me for the pillowcase then," Tinsley said. "I didn't know that was a crime."

"Makes sense that they would charge you for the missing pillowcase, doesn't it? After all, you were the one paying for everything. That must have been infuriating, Tinsley. I know I'd be livid if someone stuck me with the bill for that ridiculous party, especially if I had a low-paying job like yours."

Tinsley scoffed. "I'll say it again for you, detective. Nice and clear. I. Didn't. Kill. Mara."

"The real question is—why did she try to kill you, Tinsley?" the detective asked.

Tinsley flinched at the words.

The detective lifted a hand and motioned at someone in the mirror behind her. Moments later, two detectives entered the room.

"Don't worry. We're not arresting you. I just want to see the back of your head," the detective said.

Tinsley rolled her eyes and leaned forward on the desk. "Fine. Be my guest." The detectives stood behind her as she slowly parted her hair down the middle.

One of the detectives winced, the other made a hissing noise through his teeth.

"You'd better come look at this," he said to Detective Smalls.

Around the desk and behind her suspect, Detective Smalls moved to inspect Tinsley's wound.

A deep gash, crusted over with blood and debris and nearly two inches long, lays hidden beneath her hair.

"My god, Tinsley. That thing needs stitching up."

"I'm fine," Tinsley huffed.

As the detective took her seat, one of the technicians snapped photos of the wound. Tinsley glared angrily at the detective, quickly shifting her hair back into place when they were done with their pictures

"Make sure you tag me in that on Facebook, yeah?" she said, smirking at the young technician.

The detective didn't react to Tinsley's joke. Despite her attempt at humor, the injury looked incredibly painful.

"Are you a big reader, Tinsley?"

This time, Tinsley opened her mouth and laughed. "Is reading a crime now, too?"

The detective shook her head. "It's only a matter of time before we find out that it's your blood on the book, and on the pillowcase that you tried to hastily hide away in the bush out back by the pool."

"The book fell on my head, okay? It was on the top shelf and those books are heavy as fuck. I was embarrassed. And I'm tougher than I look, so I'll be okay."

The detective shook her head from side to side. "Nope. Try again. Unless that book lifted itself off the floor, swung back, and bashed you a second time, then there's no way it happened the way you just said it did."

Tinsley spread her hands out on the desk, flexing her fingers. Open and closed. Open and closed.

"Who hit you over the head with that book, Tinsley? And why are you covering for them?"

"I'm not covering for anybody," she snapped, curling her fingers into tiny fists.

"Was it Mara? Is that why you pushed her off the balcony?"

Tinsley's eyes grew wide, shoulders stiffening.

"I'll unravel it all on my own eventually, so why don't you just save me the trouble and the time? I can help you, Tinsley. But only if you talk to me."

Tinsley leaned back in her chair, slouching down. Gingerly, she reached back and touched the wound on her head and winced.

"It must have hurt like hell."

"She wasn't a good person, okay?"

"Who wasn't?" the detective prodded, moving to the edge of her seat.

"Mara. She took advantage of me when it came to paying for the party, sure. But it went way beyond that…"

"Okay. Why don't you tell me then? I'm all ears," the detective said.

"I didn't like her from the start. And I don't just mean during the party planning phase. She and Rosalee became friends in college. At first, she was all Rosalee talked about. I was a little jealous, but mostly I was happy for her. I care about Rosalee; she's less like a cousin, and more like a sister to me. Do you understand?" Tinsley said, finally softening as she discussed her painful feelings toward her cousin.

The detective nodded, waiting for more.

"I tried to go visit. I tried to call. But every time, her stupid friend Mara got in the way. She answered Rosalee's phone most of the time. Never passed on my messages. Rosalee was always 'out', or 'busy'. I wondered back then if Mara was controlling, but Rosalee's a grown woman and I had my own life to live."

"Of course, you did. That's understandable," the detective said.

"When we started planning the party, I liked Mara

even less. She seemed shady as hell to me and when she kept dodging me about the money, I decided to do a little investigating of my own. I talked to a couple of her old roommates and even reached out to her current roommate."

"What did you find out, Tinsley?"

Tinsley frowned. "She hadn't paid her rent in nearly six months. She was basically squatting there and refusing to leave. And her roommate had a lot to say about her... Apparently, she was scamming people for money online. Using phishing software in some cases, bribing married men out of money. Like I said, she wasn't a good person. She basically survived by taking advantage of and hurting others."

"Did you tell Rosalee about any of this?" the detective asked.

Tinsley shook her head. "I doubt she would have listened. She's naïve sometimes."

"Perhaps you should have been honest and let her decide for herself. She's smarter than you give her credit for," the detective said.

"Perhaps," Tinsley shrugged. "But the tables soon turned when Mara found herself on the other end of a scam. Her own computer was hacked, the small amount of money she did have drained. All of her accounts taken over by bots, credits cards racked up in her name."

"And who did that?"

Tinsley smiled and shrugged once again.

"You're smart, Tinsley. I'll give you that. But you don't strike me as the computer genius type."

Tinsley sat back in her chair and started picking at her cuticles, seemingly bored with the conversation now. Acting wasn't one of her strong suits either. The detective picked up on her anxiety from a mile away.

"Is that why she hit you? She found out it was you?"

Tinsley sighed and kept picking at her nails.

Finally, she said, "After the lights went out, I decided that it was the perfect time to confront her. I wanted her to admit the truth so that I could eventually expose her to Rosalee. To everyone. Not only did she try to kill Georgia with that whole coconut thing, but she'd been taking advantage of people and making others miserable with her scheming. I was going to expose her, possibly even turn her into the authorities. I wanted to see the look on her face when I told her I knew everything."

"And did you confront her?" the detective asked.

"Yeah. I tried to make it a little fun. I knocked on her door and told her to meet me downstairs so we could talk. Then, I waited in the kitchen until I heard her in the hall, and I flipped the breakers off. I wanted to give her a scare, but it was me who got it worst of all. I walked into the library, and it was so quiet. She was moving around and saying my name, but I just kept silent for a couple minutes to freak her out. I think she thought I was a ghost moving in there or something! And then I told her that I knew all about the fraud. I listed off people and companies she had hacked. I told her she was finished and that I was going to file a police report and make sure no one got duped by her ever again..."

"That must have really pissed her off," the detective said.

Tinsley's lips curled. "I knew she would respond angrily, but I didn't think she'd try to kill me over it. Such a disgrace... I'm the ultimate book lover and I basically got beat over the head with something I love more than anything. If I were going to be murdered, that wouldn't be the worst way to go..."

"I don't understand why you didn't call the police, Tinsley. She could have been locked up for assault and battery, right then and there," the detective said, spreading her hands questioningly.

Tinsley frowned. "Yeah, like anyone would have believed me anyway. Death by book, and all that. Plus, I didn't get the chance to. I was stunned, lying on the floor for nearly an hour afterward. I think I might have even blacked out for a bit. Nobody came looking for me. Nobody came to help. I woke up in the library. The door was closed. When I came out of the room, the house was quiet. Everyone was asleep, I guess. I went upstairs and collapsed in bed. She wasn't hanging from the rafters when I came out of the library and that was like 2:30 a.m.

I tried to lie down and rest, but an hour later I heard people screaming downstairs. I sat up and noticed blood on my pillowcase. I was panicking at first, unsure if the screams were real or in my head..." Tinsley explained.

"But why did you hide the pillowcase outside if you weren't guilty of killing Mara? That makes no sense. I'm sorry, but it doesn't."

"Because I didn't hide it until after," Tinsley said, with a frown.

"After?"

"After we walked in and found her hanging. I knew I'd look guilty. If anyone had a reason to kill that bitch, it was me. And I didn't want to get blamed for her suicide either. Part of me hoped that she felt so guilty and awful... that she had decided to take herself out. But I should have known better. No way that conceited bitch would have offed herself. She was too vain for all that."

The detective pushed her chair back. Finally, some answers! "We're done for now," she said, motioning to one of her deputies.

Chapter Thirty-Two

INTERVIEW 2: SUSPECT #4

B ri took a seat across from the detective and cracked her knuckles on the table. She looked exhausted, dark circles under her eyes. Her hair looked knotted and greasy, pulled back in a tight ponytail at the nape of her neck.

"When did you first meet Tinsley?" the detective asked, folding her hands on the table neatly.

Bri's mouth opened then closed; it wasn't the question she'd been expecting.

Finally, she said, "On the first day of the p—"

The detective drummed her fingers on the table. "I don't mean in-person, Bri. Nowadays, there are so many ways to meet people, and to communicate. You don't strike me as a face-to-face person, especially considering your line of work."

"Do I need a lawyer?"

"Your brother will be here soon," the detective said, with a shrug. "You tell me. Do you?"

Bri shook her head. "Of course, I don't. I've done nothing wrong."

"Then answer the question, Bri. Because I've already woken up a few of my favorite judges and I'm getting a subpoena for your computer, all of your computers, as we speak," the detective warned.

Bri narrowed her eyes.

The detective said, "Here's what I think, Bri. I think that Tinsley found out that Mara was a scammer. Complex phishing scams, bribery... It only makes sense that she would ask her cousin's future sister-in-law who works in computers to help her dish out a little payback. I bet you could create viruses and hack into people's computers in your sleep, Bri. I did my research too. You graduated with the highest distinction. Your mother might not be overly impressed with your job, but you've got quite the reputation online. People think you're a computer genius."

Bri couldn't help herself from smiling. But then she straightened her face, tried to return the detective's knowing look with a blank stare.

"What's your point?" she asked.

"I already know it was you, Bri. I just don't

understand why you'd help Tinsley. Or why you thought murder was the answer here..."

"I didn't kill Mara," Bri said, through clenched teeth.

The detective was silent, waiting.

Finally, Bri took a deep breath and went on, "As far as Tinsley goes... I don't know her well. But you're right. She did reach out to me. And there's nothing I hate more than a scammer. I know it's hard to understand, but family means everything to me. I love my mother and my brother, and I would do anything to protect them. Rosalee might not be my cup of tea, but as long as she's part of this family, I'll protect her too. My family has a lot of money, detective. I wasn't going to let Rosalee, or my brother, get scammed by that stupid little bitch, Mara."

"But that's exactly what happened, isn't it? Only it was you who was her victim. You found out she was involved with the hackers who ripped you off last year."

"You don't know that," Bri snapped.

"No, I don't. Not yet. But I will. And it's not hard to figure out. You were scammed by someone, and Mara is a scammer. She might have been good at tricking people, but she wasn't a whiz kid like you, was she?"

Bri kept silent.

"So, you hacked her accounts and drained her money. Tit for tat. Someone had recently wiped out all her accounts and stolen her identity, that's what her roommate said. You gave her a little karma by hacking her. Then what?"

Bri threw up her hands. "Then nothing. That's all I did. I paid her a little lesson. Mara got what she deserved."

"Tinsley confronted Mara when the lights went out and Mara nearly killed her, beating her over the head with a book. You must have known that she was dangerous. How could you be so smart and also so stupid?" the detective challenged her.

Bri flashed a mouthful of clenched teeth. "I knew right away what happened with Tinsley. Mara, that evil bitch, came and told me about it herself. She was the stupid one… bragging to me about how she hit Tinsley for smarting off to her, laughing about sending Georgia to the hospital, rattling on and on about her mean little anonymous note she wrote Rosalee. She was an awful person, detective. I'm sorry to say that I don't think many people will miss her."

"So, what did you do about it, Bri?" the detective asked.

Bri let out a small laugh. "I didn't have to do anything, you see. Mara, that little arrogant fool, did it all to herself."

"Are you saying she jumped from the balcony in your room? It is your room that is directly above the spot she cracked her skull on next to the pool. I have technicians out there right now, analyzing the scene and gathering any blood evidence they can find by the pool. We're also taking a look at your balcony..."

Now it was Bri's turn to look surprised. Slowly, her shocked look morphed into something else—glee and appreciation.

"Nice work, detective. I didn't think you'd figure out the pool," she said.

"Why did you push her from the balcony? Say what you will about her character, but that doesn't justify murder. You have to know that, Bri. Deep down, you know that's not okay."

"She jumped, just like I said. I almost wish I had pushed her. She would have deserved it, trust me! But no... She jumped."

"And why the hell would she do that?" the detective demanded.

Bri shrugged. "Because I dared her to do it. I told her there was no way she could pull it off. And that arrogant little bitch tried to prove me wrong. But guess what? I'm never wrong. The trajectory made it impossible. It's simple physics, really, and it didn't take a genius to figure it out. I did a rough calculation, initial velocity and potential outcomes... To be honest, she got closer to the pool than I predicted she would. Surprised the hell out of me. But not close enough..."

Detective Smalls was on her feet now. "Bri Beake. You

have the right to remain silent. Anything you say can be used against you in court…"

"Blah, blah, blah," Bri interrupted. "You can go ahead and arrest me, but I won't serve time. I didn't push her or force her to jump into the pool. She did it all herself! I can't help it if she fell to her death, detective."

The detective grimaced. "That's just the thing, Bri. Mara didn't die from the fall. She wasn't dead on impact. We'll have to wait until the final reports come in, but there was frothy blood in her airways and water in her belly. She might have had a severe brain injury after she smacked the side of that pool, but she was breathing when she hit the water. She was *breathing*, Bri. She was alive in the pool, and you left her down there to drown. In my eyes, that makes you a killer."

Part Three

~

"It is difficult to say who does you the most mischief: enemies with the worst intentions or friends with the best."

— E.R. Bulwer-Lytoon

Chapter Thirty-Three

ROSALEE

The Wife

It was a crisp October afternoon when we said our vows, hand in hand, in the center of Merribelle Gardens. My father wasn't there to give me away and my best friend wasn't standing beside me. Nor was my sister-in-law, who had spent the better part of the last several months in jail, awaiting trial for her role in Mara's death. She and Delfina would have to answer for their crimes and be judged by a group of their peers.

Although Delfina had initially admitted to hanging the body to make it look like a suicide, she had failed to mention the pool to detectives, and she'd stopped talking to the police altogether now—at the advice of her lawyer, of course.

Most of the guests in their fancy white chairs belonged to Asher's family, friends, and co-workers. But Tinsley was there beside me. And Georgia stood with me, too.

Elizabeth Beake was front and center in the first row, watching and crying as Asher and I read our vows to one another. She smiled that day, the first real smile I'd seen from her in a long time. With Bri's future freedom hanging in the balance and the cancer eating away at her body, she had shriveled and shrunk inside herself.

At the reception, I pulled her aside.

"I wish Bri were here today. I'm sorry she isn't," I told my mother-in-law.

Elizabeth gave me a critical look. "Are you really? Because she played a role in the death of your best friend. I can't imagine that's an easy pill for you to swallow, Rosalee."

I shook my head. "Mara wasn't the best friend that I thought she was. And anyways, I would feel sad about Bri regardless. She is your daughter and my husband's sister, and I can tell that it's killing you, Elizabeth. You feel like you're losing her, just like you lost Edmund. And for that, I'm so very sorry."

Elizabeth's eyes brimmed with tears. She tried to talk, but her voice was quaky, and she waved me off.

"And I wish Edmund was here too." I reached out and took her hand in mine, giving it a little squeeze.

"Me too," Elizabeth said, her words whispery, muffled sobs.

"Bri will get off soon. You know that, right? She and Delfina have the best lawyer in the world," I said, pointing over at Asher. He was standing near the cake, holding a flute of champagne, watching me talk to his mother with adoring eyes.

"I hope so. What Bri did was so wrong, I know that. I just wish I could have shaken some sense into her, stopped her... The only solace I have is that maybe her being in jail will help her come off the alcohol and the pills," Elizabeth said.

"I hope so," I said, truthfully. "Elizabeth..." I squeezed her hand again. "I have a favor to ask you."

"Anything," she said, wiping tears from her cheeks and giving me the kindest, and most genuine smile I'd ever received from her. She wasn't the easiest person to love or deal with, but I loved her son and that meant there was a part of me that would always love her too because of it.

"I need you to take the chemo. And the radiation. Please."

"Uh-uh." Elizabeth was already shaking her head. "I'm sorry, dear. I love you both, but I don't want to go through that. I'm ready to meet my maker and be reunited with my sweet Edmund. Surely, you understand that."

"I think Edmund can wait a while," I said, taking her hand in mine and placing it on my rounded belly. "Your grandchild is going to need you. And I need you... I don't have any parents of my own. I don't want this child not to know their grandmother, Elizabeth. Please. This is important. The doctors said you have a great chance of beating this with the treatment if you start now."

Elizabeth's eyes bulged at my growing belly. "You're pregnant? This isn't some sort of joke?"

I laughed. "Of course, I'm not joking. You're going to be a grandmother. But I want you to know that this baby will have both mine and Asher's last names. I know you don't like it, but my mother's maiden name is all I have left of her. I'm not ready to give that up. And I'm not planning on having more than one or two kids, so you and Asher can just get over that whole fantasy," I said, laughing as I looked over my shoulder at my handsome husband.

He was grinning from ear to ear and could obviously tell that I'd shared the news based on the joyous, shocked expression on his mother's face. He raised his glass. Elizabeth, hands shaky with excitement, grabbed her glass and lifted it toward him.

"So, what's your answer? Will you fight to live for me and Asher? For this baby? I think Edmund can wait just a bit longer, don't you?" I asked.

Instead of answering, Elizabeth threw her arms around me. I could feel hot tears saturating my dress.

"Of course, I will, dear. It would be an honor."

"And you can help me pick out some maternity clothes. This time I actually need them," I said, with a wink.

Elizabeth closed her eyes and chuckled. I stared at her face, the laugh lines at the corners of her lips, the frown lines between her brows. She was a unique woman, with a lifetime of memories and regrets that she carried with her. As difficult as she was to get along with sometimes, I wanted to love her. And I wanted my baby to know their grandmother.

My eyes scanned the crowd, looking for familiar faces. I could see Tinsley floating through the aisles; surprisingly, she was talking and smiling. She seemed to be enjoying herself, coming out of her shell a bit. And behind the back row, where the sun cast a narrow pocket of shadows, I saw my mother. In her simple white dress, long black hair flowing like silk in the breeze, she stood watching. She smiled, lifted her hand, and waved me goodbye.

Chapter Thirty-Four

DELFINA

The help

That night...

They say that there are two sides to every story. But, in my seventy years on this earth, I've learned that there are many more than two. In the end, all that matters is truth.

I'll go to the grave protecting my truth.

It was two in the morning when I heard the shouts. The door to Bri Beake's room was flung open, the silky cream curtains I'd ironed countless times were blowing recklessly in the breeze.

You see, the butler's pantry isn't the only hidden area in the house. Both sides of the estate are equipped with tiny rooms and corridors; all in the name of keeping the 'help' hidden and out of sight. Always working on the periphery, always hidden from the heart of the house. But, unfortunately for me, the original 'help' at Leblanc-Landry had access to outhouses. There are no longer outhouses on the premises, which means I have to either take a chance of running into guests when I creep around and use the lavatories, or I have to sneak a piss out in the bushes when no one is looking.

And that's exactly what I was doing— 'popping a squat'—in the shrubbery, when all hell broke loose between Bri and Mara.

I could see them up there in Bri's room, nose to nose, and arguing vehemently. Somehow, they'd both ended up on the balcony, voices rising and carrying in the wind. I worried that someone might hear them and call the authorities. That certainly wouldn't be good for business!

I ducked further into the shadows and tripped around, trying to tug up my underwear and stiff khaki pants, worried they might spot me.

But there was no chance of that; they were too focused on each other.

I was just about to slip around the side of the house, when I saw the push. Bri, face angry as a bull, shoved the woman, Mara. Both hands pressed against her chest, not hard. But hard enough. I watched the woman tumble through the sky, as though she were a fallen angel, cast out by Jesus himself.

Mara's head made a loud, wet crack as she fell onto the edge of the pool and then there was an enormous splash as her body tumbled into the water.

Horrified, I raised a hand to cover my mouth, squelching the screams I wanted to let loose.

Slowly, I forced myself to look back up at the balcony, all the while praying that that monstrous woman wouldn't see me and kill me next.

But I was invisible to her, as her eyes were trained on the pool. Bri was grinning like a Cheshire cat, giddy with what she had done. I stood frozen on the periphery, not daring to move, until the balcony door thumped shut and the curtains swished together again.

I counted to twenty and then I crept forward, walking on my tiptoes to the edge of the pool.

Mara lay on the bottom of the pool, eyes open and wide, glassy eyes staring back at me as she uselessly tried to flail her failing arms.

I made the sign of the cross over my chest and turned to leave. After a lifetime of being invisible as a servant, I knew it wasn't my place to get involved. Even if I wanted to try to save her, I wasn't strong enough.

But that's when I saw her—Elizabeth Beake, soaking casually in the steamy hot tub. How had I missed her?

She was looking right at me, eyes round as quarters,

and she was so still that, for a moment, I worried that she, too, was dead. Finally, she moved, lifting her long, lithe, naked body from the hot pool, and she walked straight toward me.

I hate that expression, 'You could tell she was beautiful once', because it implies that you can't be beautiful *and* be old at the same time.

Elizabeth Beake *was* beautiful, probably more beautiful than she was in her youthful days. When she reached me, she took her hands and gripped both of my arms with surprising strength.

"Delfina, right?"

I nodded, glancing sideways once more to the now dead girl in the pool. She seemed to be alive on the bottom of the pool after she fell, but she certainly wouldn't be breathing for much longer…

"How would you like to make more money than you could ever dream of? Enough so that you can quit this job and do whatever you want, and still be able to leave money to all your kids and grandkids?" Elizabeth said.

I nodded again, starstruck by her confidence and wild talks of whimsy.

"Where can we hide this body? I'm sure you know a place, don't you?"

I nodded again, my lips stuck together and my tongue firmly stuck against the roof of my mouth.

"Listen to me, Delfina. We hide the body for just a

short while. Just until we can dry it off and make a plan for what happened here tonight. Let's make this look like it's something she caused herself. Perhaps a hanging death or another kind of suicide?" Elizabeth calmly suggested.

"Y-yes." I forced out the words.

"And I'll pay you lots of money to help me. Deal?"

Even if I wanted to refuse, I got the feeling I couldn't. If I'd said no, she probably would have drowned me in that hellish hot tub, or something worse.

That night, we lifted the body from the pool and carried it over to an abandoned shed at the back of the property. We might be old, but we're stronger than we look. A lifetime of raising children and working our fingers to the bone has taught us how to grunt and take it when it comes to pain.

After she was laid out in the shed, I cleaned Mara's wound and dried her hair. I dressed her in one of my old dressing gowns. Then I tracked down a piece of rope from the washing room. "You know, this is where he stacked all the bodies," I told Elizabeth, pointing at the shed.

"Excuse me? What are you talking about?" Elizabeth said, giving me a look of disgust.

"Never mind."

We worked quickly, once we knew the others were

asleep in their beds. Even Bri, the killer herself, didn't know what we were up to.

Together, we hauled the body in and propped it up, slipping a noose over its head. It took both of us to pull the rope, using the leverage to lift her into the rafters.

She looked sort of pretty, hanging there like a ghost from a forgotten era.

The police have asked me again and again which one of my staff helped me move the body, but I refused to talk. Elizabeth has offered me the best counsel that money can buy and a million dollars when I come out on the other side of this legal shitstorm. I just hope I get out soon enough so I can enjoy it. I want to move somewhere far from here, somewhere nice where people can serve my meals and clean up after me for a change.

But at this point, any place would be better than my prison cell. Hell, I'd even settle for that stupid little butler's closet I used to call home.

Acknowledgments

First and foremost, I want to thank my readers—some of you are new to me, and some of you have been around for a long time, since I was writing in the indie arena. I appreciate all of you, old and new. Thanks for taking a chance on me and my stories. I can't tell you how much it means to me that you're reading my words...

My sincerest thanks to my brilliant editors, Jennie Rothwell, Eleanor Goymer, and Dushi Horti. Your vision for this book, from the cover design to the plot to the execution to the tiniest details, was utterly invaluable. Thank you for all of your help and guidance with this story!

Thank you to my extraordinary agent, Katie Shea Boutillier. She championed this book and all of my projects, pushing for me to be the very best that I can be and advocating for me every step of the way. I couldn't do it without you, Katie! Thank you for believing in me and taking a chance on me all those years ago…

Huge thank you to all of the staff at One More Chapter and HarperCollins—the cover design made my heart soar. Thank you, Lucy Bennett! I've always wanted a cover with HOT PINK on it and you all certainly delivered. I adore the design! To the publicity team— thank you for working so hard to connect my books with the readers who love them. I see you working tirelessly behind and in front of the scenes to make our books succeed, and I can't tell you how much it amazes me!

Thank you so much to all of the librarians, booksellers, bloggers, and influencers who help champion books and connect stories like mine with the readers who enjoy them.

To my family and friends for supporting my dream, from its rocky beginning to now. I appreciate the love and encouragement. I couldn't do it without you all! Dexter, Tristian, Violet, and Shannon—I love you all so much.

To my mother, who loves New Orleans just as much or more than me… I promise to take you again someday soon. Bob Dylan was right: there are so many places I like, but New Orleans really is better!

Read on for an extract from The Secrets of Cedar Farm

Behind every family is a story. Within that story, there's always someone like me.

The black sheep. The troubled one. Resident fuck-up. Whatever you want to call it … that's me.

Sometimes the title is well-earned—we're outsiders because we deserve to be. Other times, it's for one reason and one reason only—we know too much.

Banish the person, banish the secrets…

Chapter One

STEP 1: HONESTY

"You look too young to be a widow."

It wasn't the first time I'd heard those words.

Not the first time I'd told this lie: "He died in battle."

It's a quick way to shut down questions because—let's face it—twenty-four is too young to lose your spouse, and, this way, everyone assumes he died valiantly on the battlefield, fighting whoever the powers that be designated as the current bad guy.

I tried to imagine Finn as a Viking, disgruntled and daring. His lips curled at the corners, a secret smile. *We used to share so many of those.*

"I'm sorry for your loss. Which branch did he serve in?"

Empathetic brown eyes rose to meet mine, the cab driver watching in the rearview mirror. He was handsome, fortyish. Kind. Perhaps big and strong, too, but nothing compared to my fantasy of Finn the Viking.

I sighed; the rush of breath louder than I'd intended.

This entire conversation was my fault, for correcting the driver when he referred to me as "Miss Campbell" at pick-up. It's *Mrs*. At least it should have been…

I looked out the window, glaring at the blurry rows of soybean and corn, imagining Finn's feathery lashes, the rough pads of his thumbs … and *that* laugh, the kind that requires you to laugh with your whole chest when you do it. *God, how I loved his laugh.*

Viking, he was not. But, oh how he made me smile…

Hmm … which branch did he serve in?

"Not the kind with medals and flags," I said, finally.

The marriage part was a lie too—like so many things that happened between us, I was stretching the truth.

Finn and I were engaged, not married yet, when it happened. We said we were married so often that perhaps we even believed it.

But then Finn died. And our plans, our dreams … they all died with him in the middle of our junky living-room floor on a cold winter night. Our junky house and our junkie ways… His death as inevitable as me landing here, in rural Indiana, forced to grovel with an aunt and uncle I barely knew.

Give my daughter back. PLEASE.

The driver must not have heard me, because next thing I knew, he was talking about his own father, an accomplished military pilot…

Finn died in battle.

It was *sort of* a lie. Though not really.

Finn was never a soldier, but he did, in fact, wage war.

Battling his demons, putting his body through hell in its war with opioid addiction, until his body finally threw out the white flag of defeat…

You won, Finn. Your destructive willpower outlasted the shell you were born in, just like you always said it would. And now, you'll never get the chance to make me smile or laugh again…

No more secret smiles for me.

The rest of the cab ride was silent, much to my relief.

My hands shook as I remembered the letter in my hands; the last (and only) letter Gemma wrote me while I was in rehab. *But did two sentences really count as a letter?*

I miss you. I hate it here Mom.

Those words, as much as it pained me to read them, gave me one small glimmer of hope—*Gemma still calls me Mom.*

Not her deadbeat father, not my eccentric aunt and

uncle … not my catty never-became-my-sister-in-law Jewel.

Me.

I'm Mom. And, regardless of my past mistakes, I always will be.

The driver followed a snaky paved road, past a meadow teeming with wildflowers. Rolling my window down, I drew in the heady perfume.

Nice to catch a break from the cornfields and cattle shit.

A gentle hill arose from the earth, and then the cab rattled to a stop.

"Here we are, Ma'am," the driver said, careful not to call me "Miss" again.

After hours of passing nothing but grainy farmland, smudgy patches of churches and painted farmhouses … I was finally here.

The rotting monstrosity rose before me, like a bad dream. I lowered my sunglasses, taking it all in.

The house had been beautiful once, you could tell. But the rotten, peeling Victorian that belonged to my aunt and uncle looked to be on the verge of collapse. Steeply pitched points and arched windows gave the house a gothic appeal.

Creepy.

Now this is my daughter's home, too, I thought, unable to hide my shock and dismay.

Truth was, I could barely remember Cedar Farm from

my youth, having spent so little time here. In my mind's eye, I'd imagined a cutesy farmhouse, something wholesome with chickens and ducks. Not this dilapidated, pseudo-haunted house.

But it was my aunt and uncle who had turned up at my court hearing after Finn's overdose and my third arrest. It was they who had volunteered to take custody so that Gemma didn't become a ward of the state. With my own parents dead and gone, the chances of finding an alternative to foster care had seemed slim … until my long-lost relatives showed up to save the day.

Deep down, I knew I should feel more grateful toward Sara and Francis. They had taken in my daughter, whom they had never met … and now they were offering to take me too.

You can stay with us until you're ready to bring her home, Aunt Sara had offered over the phone when I was fresh out of rehab.

But coming here, after ninety days of treatment and feeling disconnected from my daughter, all I could feel was bottled-up fear. Fear that they wouldn't give her back. Fear that she wouldn't remember how close we once were… Only seven, Gemma's resilient heart and mind might help her block me out for good…

I'm clean. I'm sober. I'm taking my meds. I'm working the program. But good luck convincing the judge of that.

And this house … it was nothing at all like what I

expected. Not where I would have wanted to leave my daughter… *But in times of desperation, I couldn't afford to be picky, could I?* And, after all, it was my own fault she'd had to come here. *I have to accept the blame for putting her in this position to begin with.*

The driver popped the trunk and handed me the skinny yellow suitcase I'd had since I was a teenager. It contained extraordinarily little—five outfits, some panties and socks, a few toiletries, and my AA bible, also known as *The Big Book*.

"Thank you, sir."

I'd paid the driver in advance online, but I knew I should offer a tip. I scrounged through my dress pockets for a five and two ones, guiltily handing over what little loose cash I had.

The driver, in a strange old-fashioned gesture, tipped his hat and took a bow before climbing back behind the wheel. Gravel dust tickled my nose and throat as he rumbled away, leaving me here alone in front of the crumbling house holding the few possessions I owned. The only thing I cared about was inside that house, my sweet daughter…

A tire swing moved back and forth, creaking in the wind. I waited for the screen door to pop open, my aunt and uncle, or (hopefully) Gemma, to emerge to greet me. But nobody came. The grumbling of tires disappeared in the distance, and suddenly, I felt very alone.

I looked left then right, taking in the vast open cornfields on either side of the house and the hulking shadow of trees beyond it... There wasn't a neighbor around for miles, I realized.

The house looked even more dilapidated as I approached, the eyes of two ghastly stone creatures leering down at me from above. This was the first time I'd seen a gargoyle in real life. It reminded me of old vampire movies, and I shivered. The home was large and historic, Victorian according to Aunt Sara, but the gargoyles seemed over the top. I tried to recall what I knew about gargoyles... *Aren't they supposed to ward off evil or something? Maybe that's not such a bad thing after all I've gone through this year,* I considered.

Although I should have remembered the house from my childhood, nothing about this place felt familiar.

I'd been younger than Gemma when Mom and I had come to visit her sister Sara.

Nothing about this place feels like it should. Most of all, my aunt and uncle themselves are complete strangers to me. I didn't even know who they were at first when they showed up in court. As grateful as I am for their help, it's obvious that my daughter isn't happy here. Her recent, snappy letter proved that.

I'd mailed out dozens of letters, all of which had gone unanswered until I'd received her short reply.

Considering how eerie and isolated it is out here, I can see why she hates it. This isn't at all what I expected. What other surprises are in store for me? I wondered, overcome with a sense of foreboding.

Steadily, I gripped my suitcase and approached the house.

I must get my daughter back, at all costs, and take her home to Chicago.

Chapter Two

The house looked out of place: this dark, Victorian monster in the middle of a desolated cornfield … almost like it had been picked up from some ancient era and dropped from the heavens above. I couldn't shake the thought that it didn't belong. But who was I kidding? *I don't belong here, either. And neither does my daughter.*

The once-white paint was peeling now, and I fought the urge to pluck a strip and peel it all the way back as I rapped my knuckles on the old screen door.

Breathless, I held on to my suitcase, fingers white and achy with nerves. I waited. Then waited some more. A flutter of excitement at seeing Gemma and anxiety at facing my relatives raced through me, making my stomach twist and curl noisily as the minutes ticked by. Like an obscene version of 'the butterflies' I couldn't get rid of… For a moment, I almost wished I'd taken an extra dose of my anti-anxiety medication on the way here. But the doctor's voice reverberated in my head: *It's important that you take your meds as prescribed. Even though these are non-narcotic, make sure you follow the dose and don't over-medicate.*

I drummed my fingers on the screen door, waiting.

When no one came, that flutter turned to something else—*what if I'd come to the wrong place? What if I'm stuck out here, this house straight out of the* Texas Chainsaw Massacre *movie, with no ride to get me back into town? Where is Gemma?*

I moved to the dusty front window and cupped my hands around my face, squinting to see in.

There was no one inside as far as I could tell, but I was relieved to see the house was better kept on the inside than the out, and there were no chainsaw-wielding weirdos.

Through the window, I could see a lavish room with Oriental rugs and the kind of furniture you'd read about in a novel, timeless and Dickensian. There was an ornate fireplace and thick wooden shelves lined with books.

The opposite of our shabby little apartment in Illinois. Six hundred square feet, the apartment had only one door in the entire unit—the arched entrance to the bathroom, that separated it from the kitchen/living room/bedroom that bled together like a heaping tumor.

As much as I complained about the lack of space and storage, I wouldn't have traded our compact place in the city for anywhere else.

Certainly not a place like this, I thought, returning to the yard to look up at the second-floor windows. The gargoyles stared back at me, eyes dark and accusatory. They were perched for flight, as though any minute now they might break free from their stony restraints.

I returned to the front door, knocking harder this time; then, finally, I left my suitcase on the porch and wove my way around the back of the property.

It was here that I caught my first glimpse of the past —the Belladonna statue, mother and daughter, and the crumbling fountain and koi pond I recognized from my childhood. In a trance, I walked straight toward one of the statues. It was streaked with lichen and crumbling, little pieces of marble clinging to the soles of my thrift store sneakers. For a moment, I was a child again ... Mom and I, racing through the yard, ducking behind statues, hair floating like kites in the wind as we played a game I liked to call "Palace Garden".

I can't believe I'd forgotten until now... How old must I have been, three or four...?

Yes, I have been here before.

I can't remember the inside of the house, but I remember these mysterious grounds ... the secrets I thought they might hold...

How strange it is that those slivers of memory come floating back in an instant, catching us by surprise...

"Norah, dear! Is that you?"

I jumped at the sound of a woman's voice, pulling my hand away from the broken, weathered nose of a sweet cherub. I hadn't heard anyone pull up, only the gentle breeze whistling between the statues, through the poorly trimmed hedges and trees. *The garden and lands were always wild. But not this rundown. Not this unkempt,* I remembered.

At the sound of her voice, I turned around. , It took me a moment to recognize her.

Sara looked like an older version of my mother, but frailer. People often said my mother had reminded them of a young Meryl Streep. I didn't see it.

Aunt Sara had long gray hair that trailed all the way down her back. But those soft green eyes that matched my mother's were patient and kind; she had that lit-from-within glow I recognized and remembered, from somewhere dark and dusty in my brain...

That day in court when she'd shown up like my last saving grace in a moment of desperation—I'd never forget it. Her eyes, so much like my mother's, had given me a small sense of ease.

"It's me. So nice to see you again, Aunt Sara." Like the driver, I felt a strange urge to take a bow or offer a curtsy. She was wearing a thin white dress and leather sandals, perfectly matched for the sticky heat of early August.

"Come here, little one."

Sara opened her arms and, surprising myself, I let her wrap me into a tight hug. It had been so long since I'd touched another person; there were strict no-contact rules in rehab between patients and staff, as well as between residents.

Aunt Sara felt light and bony in my arms, and for a moment, it reminded me ... it reminded me of Finn at the end, when he lost so much weight because of the drugs. *His collarbones sharp as daggers, his once soft belly concave. Ripples of his rib bones poking me through the sheets...*

Shivering, I stepped back from my aunt and grimaced as I shook off memories of Finn's final days. "Where's Gemma?"

A strange look flickered over Sara's face, but, in a flash, it was gone. She smiled, her big perfect teeth reminding me of my mother again.

"We just got back from having ice cream in town. I had no idea you'd be here so early."

I glanced at my watch. It was nearly five, making me a half hour late. For a moment, I wondered if we were in different time zones, and I'd made a mistake... *I'll have to check the clocks inside later, adjust my watch,* I decided.

I looked around the yard, and behind Sara, eager to see my daughter. Ninety days isn't that long, but it's an eternity when it comes to the ones you love. And, in those long months, I knew a lot could change with a seven-year-old.

"Oh, she's gone inside with Francis and little Susie. They went through the front door. They're so hyper from all the sugar and excited about their playdate."

Playdate?

"Aww, how sweet," I murmured. I'd waited so long to see Gemma; I couldn't wait a second more. I started walking toward the front of the house and Sara fell in step beside me.

"Susie is Merrill's daughter," she explained. "They're close to the same age. I thought it would be nice for Gemma to make a few family friends while she's here."

"How nice," I said. "Who's Merrill again?"

"Ah. Francis' sister. My sister-in-law. You're going to love her, I promise."

"I'm sure I will," I said, trying to hide my discomfort at the thought of sticking around long enough to get to know Francis' family. The last thing I wanted to do was try to make a long-lost connection with extended family…

Sara was my mother's sister; and although I'd met her husband Francis when I was little, I knew very little about the man. When my mother mentioned her sister in the past—which wasn't often—she rarely brought up her husband. And I didn't remember meeting him as a child either, most of my memories from that time being smudgy or non-existent...

The last time I saw them was at my mother's funeral, I realized. As though becoming a young single mother wasn't hard enough, I'd lost my own mother to cancer before the age of twenty. I wasn't used to having family support, so this whole arrangement felt beyond strange. Now, being here and seeing the creepy house and the crumbling grounds, the whole thing felt even stranger.

As we stepped over the threshold, Sara carrying my suitcase despite my protests, I took a deep breath. I was so happy to see my daughter again, but also jittery and nervous, adrenaline running through me like a live wire.

"They already went upstairs," came a gruff voice from somewhere deeper in the house.

"Francis, come see your niece," Sara scolded, motioning for me to take a seat on an uncomfortable-looking red velvet chaise lounge. Floor-to-ceiling shelves lined the walls which were filled with dog-eared paperbacks, hardcover classics, and an odd assortment of knick-knacks clogging every open nook and space. I met the glassy eyes of a dusty porcelain doll, and then my eyes drifted to a bizarre line of oil paintings on the wall.

There was a tug of recognition ... a flutter of something remembered, then lost.

The room had a dampness to it, triggering another memory ... one that was so fleeting I couldn't quite grasp it. My eyes traveled the wallpaper-coated walls and high ceilings. Despite the fancy furnishings and crown molding, there were dark water spots everywhere. *And cobwebs in the corners*, I noted, shuddering again. *Please don't let there be many spiders here.*

Moments later, a scruffy man with white hair and a beard emerged, his wide neck and shoulders taking up the entire doorway between what appeared to be the kitchen and great room.

He nodded at me, frowning. "Nice to see you again, Norah. I pray you're staying out of trouble now?" he barked.

Taken aback, I could only nod. I looked over at Sara, but her eyes were elsewhere, staring up the steep set of red-painted stairs.

"Girls! Are you ready to come down and meet our guest, Norah?" she shouted.

I stiffened. There was something strange about the way she called me a 'guest' instead of "Mom"; although perhaps that was only because she was calling out to both girls.

And why did she plan a playdate for Gemma on the same day she knew I was coming? I wondered, incredulously. I loved the idea of Gemma making friends, but this was a big day for both of us. We hadn't laid eyes on each other in months.

Also, the word "visit" perturbed me. Yes, I had come

as a temporary guest … but the plan was to take Gemma with me when I left.

I'm here for more than a 'visit'.

We still had a home in Chicago and a life to return to, and Gemma needed to be back there with her friends. Her real friends. And with me…

"Girls, answer your Aunt Sara, now!" Francis boomed, giving me another jolt.

I stood up from the lounge, smoothing my plain black dress—the only dress I owned—and cleared my throat. "It's okay, really. Why don't I just go up and see her? That way she can keep playing with her new friend," I suggested. My foot was already on the first stair when Francis said, "Wait, Norah. Let's leave them to play. Why don't we take this opportunity to chat one-on-one instead?"

"Oh." I felt a flash of irritation at having to wait even longer to see my daughter. *But I'm here now; a few more minutes of waiting won't kill me. I need to be patient and try to get along with my aunt and uncle.* Reluctantly, I followed them into an enormous kitchen and through an arched doorway that opened into a dark-paneled dining room.

Francis was already taking a seat at the head of the table. Nervously, I pulled out one of the heavy, highbacked chairs and took a seat several places away from him. The tabletop was covered in dusty bone china and bonafide napkins—the real kind, made of cloth.

There was a jaw-dropping chandelier in the center of the ceiling above the table, but like everything else, it was wobbly and stained. The whole place had an air of decay to it. A memory came floating back to me—a Dickens novel I'd read once, about a sad lady with a crusty old wedding cake rotting in the center of her dining table...

Something about this place set my teeth on edge.

Francis waited for Sara to sit down before he spoke. Once again, I tried to catch my aunt's eye from across the table, but she remained eerily quiet and standoffish in the presence of her husband.

"Now that you're here, I think it's time we lay down the rules," my uncle said, gruffly.

Chapter Three

STEP 2: FAITH

My uncle had made the rules very clear.

Some of those rules were expected: no alcohol or drugs.

Others were a little odd, but not unreasonable: no visitors, no social outings, no phone calls to friends in Chicago.

Granted, some of his rules were overreaching. I wasn't a child; rather, a grown woman, who had experienced more life lessons than most women twice my age.

It was the last rule that really bothered me: no alone time with Gemma.

At least not until we've developed some trust, my uncle had said.

In that moment, I had wanted to charge up those stairs, toss my daughter over my shoulder and run all the way home to Chicago. *Who were these people to tell me what to do? To insist on controlling my current relationship with my own daughter—the daughter I grew in my womb and raised for the first six years of her life?*

But I'd taken a deep breath and imagined myself floating on my back down the river ... the way one of my counselors at rehab taught me. If I had to play by their rules for a little while, so be it.

I wasn't innocent in all this; I'd lost custody for a good reason. *But now I'm sober and taking my mental health meds as prescribed ... what more do they want?*

It wasn't until dinner time that I saw my daughter. Feigning patience, I'd offered to help Aunt Sara in the kitchen. While she boiled potatoes and stirred stew, I peeled cucumbers for the salad.

I froze, paring knife mid-air as the tinkling sounds of children's laughter and small feet rocketing down the stairs filled the house. *Finally.*

I set the knife down, rubbing my hands on my sides, and followed the happy sounds. But as soon as I turned the corner, I came face to face with Uncle Francis. He blocked my path and turned to the girls. After his "rules" proclamation earlier, he was the last person I wanted standing between me and my daughter.

Francis boomed, "What did I say about running, ladies?"

"Sorry, Uncle Francis," the girls sang in unison.

I stepped around the hulking man to look at my daughter. Smiling, I tried to hide my surprise at the changes in her appearance. Gemma was wearing a collared white dress, stiff with starch. Vastly different from the superhero tank tops and stretchy shorts she wore at home. And her hair ... It was shorter. Much shorter. *Those bastards cut my baby's hair.*

Gemma's face broke into a silly grin and as soon as she came toward me, I was on my knees, reaching for my little girl. "Oh, angel. I missed you so much." I held her head to my chest, stroking her newly cut brown locks. *How many times had I dreamed of this moment in rehab? To smell her milky-girl skin, touch the too-soft ringlets of hair...*

Gemma had always been so fond of her long curls, that it seemed strange that she would want to cut her hair so short. But maybe she had changed her mind... *After all I've been gone from her life for three months. What do I know, really?*

I leaned back so I could see her better, cupping her sweet cheeks in my hands. Running my fingers through her sweet, brown curls. The haircut suited her face, with its delicate elfin features and wide green eyes that matched mine and my mother's. *They match Sara's too*, I realized.

"I missed you too, Mommy." As Gemma spoke, I noticed that she had lost both her front teeth. *Oh, how much I have missed over these last few months*, I thought, sadly.

I don't care what anyone says. Being an addict doesn't necessarily make you a bad parent. I still loved my daughter and had cared for her every day, until ... until the drugs took over completely.

I was a good mother once. *I'll be an even better mother this time...*

"How have you been?" My voice shook with grief and emotion.

Gemma shrugged. Another brunette stepped up beside her, looking back and forth between us, curiously.

"And you must be Susie," I smiled. Susie was pale, her skin translucent, blue veins peeping through her eyelids and cheeks. The young girl nodded, shyly.

"No more drugs?" Gemma asked, catching me off guard.

My face fell and immediately I looked over at Francis to confirm my worst fears. *Did they really tell my seven-year-old daughter about my drug use? How dare they?*

Francis merely shrugged.

"No more, I promise," I whispered, eyes wet as I pulled Gemma in for another hug.

"Come along now, my silly goose. You don't want to miss supper." Sara, who I hadn't even noticed had joined us, placed a firm hand on Gemma's shoulder. I watched as she steered my daughter away to the dining room.

Susie gave me a small, timid smile then ran after them.

"You told her?" I whisper-shouted, turning to Francis, who was still standing watchfully by the chaise lounge. "I thought we agreed that she was too young. I told her I was feeling ill, that I had to go away for a little while until I felt better…"

He crossed his arms over his chest. "We didn't actually agree on anything, Norah. And I'm fairly sure she already knew. That sort of behavior isn't something you can keep hidden. Surely you know that by now…"

My uncle walked off, leaving me standing there with my mouth hanging open.

Scooping stew and bread into my mouth, I could barely taste it. My eyes lingered on Gemma, who was seated at the other end of the table beside Susie. They were whispering conspiratorially, clinking their spoons together, and there was a warm, satisfied feeling in my chest as I watched her playing like a happy little girl, as she should be.

Sure, my aunt and uncle might be a little strange and old-fashioned … and they cut my daughter's hair and told her more about my recovery than they probably should have … but at least they had provided her with a safe home while I worked on getting better.

I tried to force myself to relax, to feel gratitude, as I finished off my supper in silence.

But as much as I tried to convince myself that I should feel grateful, I couldn't shake the feeling of unease. The house was rundown, and my uncle was strict. *But could it be that he was just old-fashioned? And the house was quaint and rural, albeit crumbly and isolated…*

No matter how desperately I wanted to feel good about this place and these people, I couldn't deny my unease.

All I wanted to do was take Gemma aside and talk to her one-on-one. She'd written that letter about hating it here, and I wanted to know why exactly. I wanted to talk to her. To run outside and play, to hold her in my arms and cuddle her like we used to in our apartment on nights before our whole life was ripped apart … to apologize for being gone all these months…

Trust. My uncle's words from earlier floated back to me as I gathered up my dinner dish and reached for my aunt and uncle's plates too. *He said that I need to earn their trust, which isn't wholly unreasonable…*

"Oh, dear. You don't have to do that," Sara said.

"I know, but I want to. You made a lovely meal. The least I can do is wash up." After I'd cleared their plates, I cleared Gemma and Susie's too. I was disappointed when Gemma jumped right up and took off back up the stairs with Susie.

At least she's adjusting well, I thought, as I gently piled the dishes in the sink.

Finn was not her father, but she'd known him and grown close to him over the last two years… *A terrible idea, on my part—bringing someone new into our lives.*

And she knew he was gone forever.

Initially, I'd thought bringing Finn into our lives was a good thing for both of us. *Oh, how wrong I was.*

I became pregnant with Gemma at seventeen; the father, a boy I went to high school with. He was never involved, opting to leave for college less than a month before Gemma was born. So, her biological father was a deadbeat and the one man she'd seen me with was dead. The last thing I wanted to do was create any more trauma in Gemma's life. Taking her back home to Chicago needed to be a smooth transition, as easy on her as possible. My aunt and uncle were right about that, even if they weren't what I was expecting.

Gemma deserves a mother who is healthy and sober. She deserves a happy home with me and her, no one else this time.

Determinedly, I scrubbed the heavy soup pot with a mesh sponge. My aunt and uncle's rules were ridiculous, surely they wouldn't make me keep to them?

I'd do whatever it took to win them over. *How hard could it be to gain their trust?*

Chapter Four

When the dishes were done and the food was all cleared, I seized the opportunity to excuse myself.

"If it's okay with you, I think I'll retire to my room. Unpack, maybe take a shower…"

Aunt Sara stood with her back pressed to the counter, a dainty cup of tea in both hands. Uncle Francis had disappeared after the plates were cleared; he seemed like the kind of man who considered cooking and clearing up to be 'woman's work'.

"That sounds fine, dear. Your suitcase is still in the library," Sara said. By library, I presumed she meant the dusty sitting room at the front of the house with all the books and creepy decorations.

I'm not sure why I expected her to escort me to my

room; there was something so antiquated about this visit, this house, that I'd almost come to expect it.

"Your room is upstairs. Second door on the left." Sara's eyes were glossy and distracted, and the way she held onto that teacup, as though it were the only thing keeping her still, reminded me of my own mother, jittery and nervous-like in the kitchen of our childhood home.

They'd been close once, Sara and my mother, Beth, before my mother's diagnosis. Over the years, I'd practically forgotten they existed. *Until they showed up to rescue Gemma.*

Part of me wanted to ask her then, about her and my mother's childhood. I never expected to lose my mom so young. *There are so many things I wish I had learned about her, so many questions to ask before she went…*

But I didn't ask Sara or bring up my mother. A part of me felt tired and strange, like an animal in a new habitat. Ninety days doesn't seem very long, but I'd grown accustomed to my life at the center—the routines, the meetings, the food, the isolation … *wash, rinse, repeat.*

Also, I didn't want to grow too attached to this place; to become too ensconced in this family. *I'll be leaving soon*, I reminded myself. *Maybe it's better if I don't ask too many questions while I'm here…*

"Thanks again for letting me come, and for watching over Gemma while I was away," I said, softly. Sara nodded, but she was still far away and dreamy, and I wasn't certain she had heard me.

In the library, I scooped up my luggage and made my way toward the steep red staircase. The girls were still playing. I could hear the shuffle and whir of toys on hardwood, and laughter like Christmas bells floating from the rooms above.

Grateful for another moment with my daughter, I started climbing. But before I made it halfway to the top of the staircase, Francis bellowed from somewhere in the belly of the house, "Girls! Time to come downstairs. Susie, your mom will be here any minute! And Gemma, you need to finish your homework and get ready for school tomorrow..."

School. I knew they had signed her up for first grade at the local public school, and I prayed she wouldn't miss her newly made friends when I transferred her back to school in Chicago. *We have so much to talk about, details to work out ... and oh, how much I have missed. My daughter's first day of first grade, a moment I'll never get back...*

I sighed, reaching the landing just as the girls came bounding down a narrow hallway, straight toward me.

Susie flew on by me, tiny feet pounding the steps in a hurry to greet her mom. Gemma was set to follow, but she stopped beside me on the landing. She had grown taller, I noticed, her cheek at my hip-level now, and she grabbed onto my leg and squeezed so hard, like she never wanted to let me go.

"Oh, sweetheart." Again, I dropped down on my knees to see her, pulling her in for a tight squeeze. "I'm so happy to be here with you and I'm sorry I was gone for so long."

"Me too, Mommy." Her eyes darted toward the staircase. I could hear Francis somewhere down below, asking Susie where Gemma was. *Why does he seem so controlling? Am I being paranoid or is he really this ridiculous?!* I wondered.

"I got the letter you sent," I told Gemma. "Why do you hate it here?"

Gemma's eyes widened for a moment, and again, she glanced down the stairs, waiting for Francis to appear.

"I don't. I was just missing you when I wrote it, is all," Gemma said, breathily.

"I know, sweetie, and I'm sorry you had to stay here for so long. I'm hoping we can go back home soon…"

"Norah." This time when Francis spoke, his authoritarian tone was directed at me. He stood at the bottom of the stairs, hands resting on his broad hips.

"Go on, Gemma." I nudged the small of her back and watched her tiny legs as she pumped down the stairs toward Francis. He opened his arms, scooping her up when she reached the bottom. As Gemma giggled, his eyes lingered over her shoulder, pinpointing mine.

There was something cruel and territorial about those eyes... I turned away from him, clutching my suitcase in one hand, flexing my fingers into a fist with the other.

There was something about the way Francis interacted with Gemma that put me on edge. And, although I'd only been here for a couple hours, I was already wary.

To complain, or even to think bad thoughts about my aunt and uncle, felt like ingratitude at its finest. If it weren't for them, Gemma probably would have become a ward of the state, I reminded myself. *I'm grateful, I'm grateful, I'm grateful...*

But I simply couldn't shake the feeling. *Something about Francis ... isn't right. Grateful or not, he's only her temporary guardian and he's acting like he's king of the castle.*

Like the ornate furniture with its semi-hidden layer of dust, and the damp chill that permeated the air, there was something rotten about my uncle, and perhaps the entire place.

The Secrets of Cedar Farm **is available in ebook and paperback now**